Suicide By Death

Suicide By Death

Mark Anthony Waters

Dedication and acknowledgment

For my sister and niece: young voices silenced way too soon. Also, to my wife, who taught me bravery and survival.

I also wanted to thank a few others. Thanks to Donna G Omo, MA, MFT, RAS for her help with details of the therapeutic scenes in the book. Donna has thirty years' counseling experience and is a licensed marriage and family therapist. Donna is also a registered addiction specialist.

Bill Barnier has been a friend and cheerleader who stepped in for a final round of editing. His honesty and forthrightness helped tighten up the book. Bill is a columnist and free-lance editor.

To round out the list, my lead editor, Carla Michale Clark. Carla helped give my main character a voice, and in a weird way, the two became friends, and in her words, "If Clair can do it, so can I." She also wrote the Epilogue for the book... please read it. Carla is an award-winning journalist and free-lance editor.

Foreword

Mark Anthony Waters has written a book that will stare you in the face. As you read, it will take you into the mind of someone whose life no longer has meaning or purpose. Suicide by Death hopes to give the reader a better understanding of suicide, attempts at it, and maybe a few answers for the survivors of a loved one who succeeded. Mark has done his research and has brought that knowledge to combine it with his personal experiences into the story.

The book is frank and honest, and some of it with a hint of dark humor. As the reader starts into this story, the lingering question early on, is, "Does she, or doesn't she?"

While reading Suicide by Death to prepare the foreword for his book, I cheered the main character on, then in the same breath, yelled at her to get help. I believe you will feel the same way. In my book series, "The For Keeps Series," the main character's sister is an alcoholic and drug addict. I also cheered her on with every keystroke hoping she wouldn't take another drink or take more drugs. She drank and partied to drown the pain after being raped as a young teen: I was nine. She did this again… again… and again, and then some more. Mark's character tries to deal with the demons that taunted her; unfortunately, my sister didn't.

I hope Mark's book might give strength to those who have lost a friend or loved one to suicide. I pray for those thinking about hurting or killing themselves or those who have tried. Suicide by Death might provide a promise that there can be better tomorrows with the right help and support.

Be prepared for an emotional journey like his first novel, Three Days in Heaven. Once again, Mark's book brings a serious topic into the light to be examined with down-to-earth writing that puts a physical human and surroundings into your mind from the words you read.

Blessings to everyone who goes down this journey and all who need help… be brave… ask.

G. M. Skovlund-Author 'The For Keeps Series.'

Introduction

How many times have you thought about killing yourself? One, two, ten? Every single day? It must have crossed your mind at some point. Wishing you were dead or had never been born, are both suicidal thoughts by any other name. So, if you said you've never once attempted suicide or at least thought about it— you're lying to yourself. Suffering, pain, and doubt were the first things many of us learned; so why wouldn't we at some point want to wish ourselves dead? With all the pressures in life and sundry setbacks along the way, for many, "checking out" a little earlier than scheduled seems like a practical alternative.

Many have convinced themselves that there are no rainbows left in the sky, and the greener grass on the other side does not exist. Others lost someone so close it seemed pointless to go on without them. Regrettably, everything that has been cited is reason enough for some to end their life. But wait, there is one more: the ultimate and final gotcha. Their shift was done; it was time for someone else to take over. Some will read this and know what I mean.

I have had my fair share of suicides in my life: distant relatives, friends, and acquaintances. One hit too close to home: the death of my sister. It was very painful and came without warning, and I learned the hard way about suicide first hand. I recently turned sixty and at a point in life when people around my age group are dropping like flies. Some of them were sick and dying, and the rest are buying Centrum

Silver by the case to prolong the inevitable. But suicide, that's a whole new ballgame.

I used to believe suicide was a coward's way out, and others continue to share that sentiment. My sister's death put me on a path of a deeper understanding, and I hope to shed light on this touchy subject.

I thought the odds were beaten and deceived myself into thinking lightning never strikes twice, but sadly it struck again; this time, it was my niece. If I had enough cynical presence of mind, I would have bought a lottery ticket. The truth is, I would have sawed off my arm with a dull blade to have been able to talk them out of it. But, in reality, and as hell-bent as they were, there were no blades dull enough to stop them, and alas, I don't own a time machine.

Most will leave a dramatic note or sometimes a voice recording for loved ones. In my sister's case, she wrote three letters. One for whoever found her (she went to a nearby lake and shot herself in the chest). The second was for the police, exonerating her spouse for having anything to do with it. The third was to her husband that included a lot of crap —most of it lies. "I'll always love you,"—she didn't. "I didn't mean to do this,"—yes, you did. "Take care of the kids,"—he did not. She left behind a little girl, five, and a boy, seven. Photos of them surrounded her body, and some lay in her lap. I suppose she thought the world would be better off without her, when in fact, it isn't. Whatever pain she suffered was over in an instant, for the rest of us, it lingers for a lifetime, and at that moment when she blew her heart to smithereens, a piece of mine went with it. I miss her every day.

In death, and I suppose other emotional trauma, the experts say most experience five stages of grief; denial, anger, bargaining, depression and acceptance. When there is a suicide, I believe the first three come all at once, and bargaining doesn't even count. How could it? And last on the list is acceptance. That's a toughie.

Some have questioned the title, Suicide by Death. At first, I thought it was cute —sort of an artsy thing, but in the back of my mind, I knew what it meant. For anyone who saw the movie Star Trek: Wrath of Khan, near the end Mr. Spock rescues the ship but sacrifices his life.

Captain Kirk runs to Spock to save him and tries to open a fuel chamber. Dr. McCoy, "Bones," said it would flood the compartment with radiation, and he and Scotty restrained the captain. Kirk struggled to free himself and murmured, "He'll die." Scotty replied in his thick, Scottish accent, said, "Sir, he's dead already."

He wasn't dead yet and had enough time to share a personal moment with Kirk, but the fact remained that Spock was on his way out; death only needed to catch up.

Folks rarely pick up a gun and blow their brains out on a whim. It takes an amount of planning. And so it begins. You have already committed suicide in your mind; it simply needs to be followed up with a bullet, noose, jump off a skyscraper or whatever; then death's bitter door swings wide open and welcomes you.

It is a safe bet that almost everyone has had to deal with suicide in their lives, and if you haven't, you'll just have to wait your turn.

My book, Suicide by Death, is not intended to be a self-help guide, though it might be. It is a fictional novel based on true events in and around my life and the lives of others. The story and its characters are broken and jagged, the language is raw, but it is real. Heck, darn and oh shoot, don't seem to have the same punch as their crude counterparts, so if you are offended, try to get over it; the message is far greater than the language.

I'd love to hear your thoughts: www.MarkAnthonyWaters.com

"Do not just slay your demons,
dissect them and find what they've been feeding on."
The Man Frozen in Time

Chapter I

At midnight, the grandfather clock announced the time. It was old, worn and grossly out-of-tune, but never missed a beat.

Ding, dong, — clang. It repeated itself twelve times representing each hour.

Trying to compete with the noise, the young mother's wailing cries echoed throughout the house.

"Curtis! Wake up! My water broke!"

Startled, her husband woke from a deep, restful sleep. The sound of the clock with its irritating melody, combined with yells from his wife, confused him in his state of absolute tranquility. In the near dark, he tried to untangle himself from the covers to rescue whatever was in distress. Instead, he fell to the floor with a heavy thunk.

She'd been awake for a while and spent the time cleaning herself, then gathered a few toiletries from the bathroom.

With the continued dinging, donging and clanging, she yelled again.

"Curtis! Did you hear me?"

Unscathed, other than his pride, he mumbled, "Dammit to hell. Again? What? What is it? Another false alarm?"

He conjured a deep, surprised response while lying on the floor.

"What do you mean your water broke?"

Panicked, she flipped on the glaring bedroom light and packed a small leather suitcase.

"The baby's coming. We have to get to the hospital… now!"

Cinderella thought she had it tough, this was no match.

The clock went silent, and Curtis lifted himself from the floor, jumping on one foot attempting to put on his pants… hiding and stifling a yawn so she wouldn't see. Curtis scratched his head in confusion, though he shouldn't be —it had been this way the entire length of the pregnancy; one problem after another. Groggy, he staggered around to find a shirt, socks, and shoes.

Digging through the dresser, he said, "I thought you weren't due until July."

"I was."

Worried and concerned, she reached for her husband's hand. Swollen with a baby and in pain, took a moment and dropped to her knees. Curtis stood by his wife. She let go of his hand, clasped hers together and prayed.

"Please, Lord, don't let the baby come too early."

Ignoring her prayers, he blurted out, "Have you seen my tie?"

Forgoing her sincere prayer, she went from the holiness of a saint to a woman from the underworld in two seconds flat.

"Forget the damn tie!"

She reached for the dresser and pulled herself up from the floor and returned to her small suitcase, snapped it shut and waddled toward the door.

"We have to go."

This whole ordeal seemed like a sign of things to come for the yet unborn child.

They arrived at the hospital within minutes and rushed her to delivery. Her husband was at her side but whisked away and ordered to the waiting room.

In those days, women's rights were not a topic, and the hospital delivery room was a metaphor for that sentiment. It was cruel at best, barbaric at worst. Fathers were never allowed in or near the delivery room. Any communication about the progress was only back and forth communication with an orderly or nurse. The doctors were gods and never questioned, and the patient intuitively remained subservient.

All the humiliation and embarrassment young women went through to have a baby, almost made motherhood not worth the trade. At most hospitals, there is a psych ward somewhere around, and I'm certain many of these new mothers got to spend a few days there.

After several hours of labor, it was time. The baby was as eager to come out as much as the mother was to keep it in.

The doctor was in position and gave the final order.

"Push!"

She strained and screamed so loud that her husband heard the cries all the way down in the waiting room. He paced back and forth and was biting his fingernails down to the nub. The screaming stopped, and all he heard was an unnerving silence —followed with more nail biting.

The baby saw its first ray of light, but lifeless.

"We have a blue baby!" cried a nurse.

The doctor cut the cord and took the infant over to a nearby warmer and did a quick assessment, swept the mouth and suctioned the nostrils. He removed his surgical gloves, and like rubber bands, shot them into a wastebasket.

"That's all I can do. Nurse, call me if anything changes."

"Yes, doctor. We will get the mother ready to move."

"Good. And you," — pointing to an orderly — "clean up this mess."

"Yes, sir."

The doctor glared at him.

"Sorry. Yes, doctor."

"That's better."

As soon as the doctor left, a nurse muttered, "What an asshole."

After some tense moments, the baby's skin tone returned to normal, then the nurse offered comforting news.

"Don't worry, everything is fine. The cord may have gotten tangled around the neck."

An aide leaned in close to the new mother and added, "He may be a jerk, but he wouldn't have left if there was a problem."

Another nurse finished cleaning the newborn, and the mother asked, "May I hold my baby?"

"In a few minutes. I need to dress and wrap her."

"Her?"

"Yes, Mrs. Reynolds, you had a little girl."

That was the first time she got the news the baby was a female.

The smell of ether lingered, and Mrs. Reynolds was still woozy from its effect and laid flat on blood-stained bedding. The nurse fluffed her pillow then placed the baby on her chest.

"Be careful, she's delicate and weak. You can have a few minutes, then we have to take her away."

She cradled and gently stroked her hair, then whispered, "Hello, Clair. Happy birthday."

Two of the nurses were mothers themselves and shared a moment of joy with Mrs. Reynolds, but that joy was soon interrupted. While the nurses were celebrating, a tech entered the delivery room with some test results, and it revealed the baby was Rh incompatible, meaning the newborn's blood type was positive; the mother's, negative. It can be a lethal cocktail.

Everyone was quick into action, including the doctor who returned to handle this emergency. Treatment options were limited in those days, and many newborns died because of it. Clair showed symptoms of anemia and was becoming jaundice. To avoid further damage, the doctor ordered a blood transfusion and took Clair away from her mother. Two hours later, they sent Clair to another room for the procedure. Not a pleasant way to start day one.

With the transfusion complete, all that remained was an empty bottle of blood still hanging above the young patient. The IV needle was removed leaving a few drops of blood behind on her tiny arm.

Clair got introduced to the world with little fanfare, but came a few weeks early, and by all standards in Nineteen-fifty-seven was premature.

She remained in critical condition for several days, and her chances of making it out of the hospital remained thin. The troubles she endured, literally began at birth, but fought and won her first of many battles to come. She learned as an infant the skills to survive, and it would be those skills Clair employed for the years that lie ahead.

The best picture, "Around the World in Eighty Days" got the Hollywood nod, and Elvis Presley was "all shook up" the year Clair was born. The best picture and top song seemed symbolic for what was to become her life. She was shaken emotionally and instead of an eighty-day trip; her resolve took many years.

Chapter II

Clair was an only child, except for her brother.

She had an upbringing like everyone else; nice house in a nice neigh-borhood, on a street with other nice houses with other nice neighbors. But in silence, there was an abundance of torment from a distant and domineering father, and an arrogant, head stuck in the sand mother. Three months after she came home from the hospital, it wasn't long before the "new car smell" began to wane.

Her father was an insurance salesman; mother stayed at home and treated her like an interruption and nothing more. The relationship with her mother was strained even as a young girl, and she never understood why. Psychologists might argue it was jealousy. Any at-tention Clair's father had for his wife, shifted away and placed on a stranger. Shortly after birth, an aunt was overheard saying that her father adored her and told everyone he knew that she looked like a little doll. To counter the adoration, her mother reminded Clair many times she was "an accident," which was a polite way of saying "not wanted." The affection her father once had, soon wore thin; she felt more like a pet than his daughter, but he still thought it was cute when she learned to walk and talk.

Years later Clair commented, "Yeah, like a trained parrot."

Clair had an older brother who had quite the reputation with the ladies, some younger than Clair. Edward was spawned by Satan himself, but to say he was evil, would have been a compliment; he was beyond evil.

Edward was fourteen and remained out in the world, 'feeling his oats' as some would say. Her idiot parents weren't aware of his 'goings on,' but heard rumors. At eight years old, Clair would be his next victim. She became part of the nourishment from his wicked feed trough and a target of his sick love interests.

Clair was on her way home from school one day, and a pack of older grade school girls approached her.

Their leader, Lucy, moved in close, and with a snarled lip asked, "How's your brother the lover?"

"Huh?"

Clair didn't understand the meaning or what it suggested.

"I have to go now."

She skipped down the sidewalk, then turned, smiled and waved.

"Bye-bye, Lucy."

On the way home, she hummed the Happy Birthday song. It wasn't her birthday, but she loved the tune. Her little dress floated, and her blond, pig-tailed hair swung back and forth with each skip.

Halfway to her destination, Clair stopped for a moment, confused and wondered, "Why is he my brother the lover? Oh well," then skipped the rest of the way home.

At the time Lucy made the comment, Edward had not touched Clair, only the others. Though she didn't understand its meaning, her time was running short and was close to finding out.

As Clair got older, she continued to live with confusion, but in her world, everything seemed normal and had no way of gauging the difference. As a young teen, and a consequence of that confusion, the relationship with her father, what little they had, drifted further apart, and again, she never knew why.

"Does he love me? Does he care?"

If he did, it didn't show.

Clair would see a father holding his little girl's hand, witnessed their happiness and said to herself, "I wish he was my daddy."

Mr. Reynolds traveled for his company, sometimes weeks at a time, and never attended a single tennis tournament or school play. After a while, whatever disappointment she felt, over time, disappointment had no meaning. They were more like strangers, and it was most evident after the abuse from Edward. It was as if he knew but never said a thing. The thought he might have known and did nothing hurt her. Some of those memories she could recall, but most remained tucked away in a fog, and any love lost between them was now resentment.

* * *

At seventeen, soon after graduating high school, Clair moved out and got her own apartment miles across town away from her family. Edward still lived at home and was useless. The scorn toward her brother was an understatement and hated they breathed the same air.

Clair was not wealthy by any means but took care of herself with the help of a small trust fund her grandmother left her and two cousins. She also had a part-time job and sold a few pieces of her art for a few bucks, mostly to friends and relatives.

* * *

It was a chilly, fall day, complimented with an occasional thunderstorm with flashes of lightning filtering through the windows. It was perfect weather to work on one of her paintings. Clair had been pondering what direction her current project was heading and studied it for hours. Interrupting her thoughts, the phone rang and took the call.

Hearing it was her brother, she asked in a deliberate and sarcastic tone.

"Yes, Edward, what do you want?"

He announced that their dad was dead, and said, "Dad is dead," then hung up.

She laid the phone down, dropped in her chair, and allowed those three words to wash over her. Clair's emotions seemed limited to only three: mad, sad and angry. She was hard-pressed to figure out which one and hadn't a clue how to react.

The first thing to pop into her head was, "*Wow.*"

There was only one hospital in the area and figured that was where they would have taken him. When Clair arrived, she asked the volunteer at the information desk where Mr. Curtis Reynolds could be found.

She punched a few keystrokes on the computer and pointed.

"He is all the way down the hall in emergency. When you get there, I'll buzz you in."

As Clair walked away, all the volunteer could say was, "I'm very sorry, ma'am."

Clair stopped, turned and looked at her. There wasn't much to say except to tell her thanks.

"What can you say at a time like this?"

And tucked way down deep inside, her next thought was eerily reminiscent of her childhood.

"Who knows, who cares."

She got to the entrance, heard the door unlock, then slammed open the swinging double doors like she owned the place. Within a few steps, she heard voices coming from the first room on the right. It was a grieving room, and Clair found her mother and brother embracing each other. Clair walked passed them and went to the E.R. intake desk instead and asked what happened. It was reported he was killed in a hunting accident.

The intake clerk knew a little about the family, and her thoughts were, "*With this crowd, he most likely jumped in front of the bullet.*"

An unsmiling nurse approached Clair.

"May I help you?"

Clair wanted to see her father, but the snotty bitch with a shitty attitude suggested, "Not now," saying it was still "quite a mess."

"Why not? Why can't I see him?"

Put out, Nurse Bitch let out a disgusted sigh.

"We'll get him cleaned up as best we can, then you can see him if you'd like."

She continued in an exasperated tone.

"But if I were you, I'd wait until the mortician straightens things out, and puts him back together. His head has more pieces than a jigsaw puzzle."

Under normal circumstances, most would be offended at such callousness, but not Clair.

"I understand. I'll just wait and see him at the funeral home."

She walked out, turned back and asked in a raised voice, "Nurse?"

"Yes, what is it?"

"Have you ever heard of Dale Carnegie?"

"No, I don't believe I have."

Clair said loud enough for all to hear, "No shit!"

* * *

The day of the funeral, the weather was still crap. It was perfect to draw and paint, but inappropriate to bury the dead —then again, maybe not. Instead of a funeral chapel with a private family room, they held it at a regular church with all the trappings; big cross, big statues, big stained-glass windows and rows and rows of pews. Family and close friends were paraded to the front ones, and Clair was the last arrival. The smell of death filled the air, and the scent of the lilies and carnations crowded her nostrils. The blend of the flowers seemed exclusive only to a funeral, leaving no doubt this was the right place. As she made her way to the assigned seating, she looked around.

"*Good crowd,*" were her thoughts, then took a seat.

Another one popped into her head, "*One down, two more to go.*"

Clair sat on the right side near an exit door, and her mother and brother sat opposite, separated by a few others. As the service was getting under way, Clair shed a few crocodile tears for her mother's sake, and by God, she leaned forward and checked. Clair also threw in two dramatic sobs to be on the safe side, then drew a sketch of the casket on the blank, back side of the program.

To be fair, Clair was shocked when she heard the news and a little sad, but most of her feelings remained stuck in neutral. She didn't pay too much attention to her father, but her eyes stayed fixed on the casket.

"That thing must have cost a fortune."

At the end of the service, she got up, marched to the front of the church and stood by her father as a show of respect, because that was what you were supposed to do. She noticed how good he looked, aside from the patch on his forehead hiding the bullet hole.

"Those ghouls did a great job," went through her mind.

Then whispered, "Let's see how good."

She was tempted to roll him over to see where it exited, but decided it might be rude.

Clair stood there a few seconds, gave him a single pat on the chest and said, "Bye, Dad. Have fun."

After saying her final farewell, she turned and walked toward her mother. She ignored Edward then stopped and said flatly, "I'm sorry for your loss."

A moment later, she retreated toward an exit.

Her mother spun around in the pew and shouted, "He was your father for Christ's sake!"

Everyone in the chapel sat in shock, but Clair kept walking and waved from behind.

"Whatever."

A few weeks after the funeral, her mother was having "one of those days," thinking of her late husband. She was sitting in the breakfast area, both elbows on the table, wine glass in one hand, a burning cigarette in the other. Clair stopped by to get a stored painters smock from her old room. Her mother looked at her as if in a hypnotic trance. A trail of dried tears lined her face, muddied by dark makeup.

She extinguished her cigarette and gulped the last of the wine.

"I wish it had been you instead of your father."

"Excuse me?"

Her mother tilted the wine glass up as high as she could to get the last drop.

"Just get what you came for and leave me alone."

Clair had nothing else to say. As requested, she gathered her things and left.

It's hard to imagine comments like that coming from a mother, but aware she was upset and blew it off. Those around them knew there wasn't any love lost between the two. Her mother later apologized despite the lack of affection. Clair accepted it with about the same amount of emotion. Though their differences separated them, the "wish it were you" comment lingered in her head, and it stung for a long time.

Chapter III

If you gathered everyone into a room and took a vote, they'd agree Clair was an attractive woman. Most would argue she was beautiful... except her. She had dark, shoulder-length hair and kept her bangs perfectly trimmed just above her eyebrows. Below her brows were deep blue eyes and a modest, athletic small frame that stood at five-feet, six inches tall. To enhance her knock-out appearance, she was also a brilliant artist. All those things Clair was on the outside, she'd look at herself in the mirror and saw sadness and nothing else. Clair longed for a prince to come save her with answers and relief. The vision hung there in silence. She gazed at the reflected image and hoped for a Snow White moment and begged that it might speak magic words. She waited, but neither one ever came; no answers or relief... and no prince. What it showed in glaring detail was the face of an abused, ashamed and broken woman. Though Clair wanted it so desperately, she was convinced there would be no 'happily ever after' for her, at least not that day... or perhaps ever.

Hunter was unmistakably handsome, but with a name like that, you must be. His features were that of a Greek god: thick blond hair, piercing green eyes, and tanned from stem to stern. With all those features going for him, instead, he had the ambition of a slow-moving snail... moving backward. Hunter barely made it out of high school, then enrolled at the local community college. He was the same age as Clair but still lived with his parents. He came home from school and announced that he wasn't cut out for college. His father was the first to speak and voiced his concerns.

"Why did you drop out?"

Hunter stood in the kitchen, munching on some leftover nachos.

"Dad, college isn't for me."

In a rare moment of fatherly advice, he said, "You should at least try it."

"I did, and I don't like it."

Now was the opportunity to be less fatherly.

"Hunter, for crying out loud, you were taking one damn class!"

"I don't want to go back, Dad! I'm not college material."

Hunter had been in and out of a few rehab centers and gone through about a dozen private counselors. He served as a constant source of embarrassment to his family, especially his father. Dropping out of college gave him another reason to ridicule his son. On one hand, he tried as best he could to be a supportive parent, but on the other, seemed to get sick pleasure out of humiliating him.

"It was your first day, idiot! Why is it so difficult for you to commit to anything?"

Then he referred to a recent rehab stay.

"Didn't they teach you anything at that loon camp?"

His father yelled each letter and every word. Charming.

"You're right, Dad, maybe I will go back and become a doctor."

"You, a doctor?" Then he laughed at him.

"Hunter, you couldn't put a bandage on a scratch."

Though these sorts of conversations were commonplace, even as a child, and as far back as he could remember, Hunter always felt "less than." His father was no cheerleader and cared more about his own success and no one else's, not even his sons.

Dr. Worcestershire was a surgeon who may have been a whiz in the operating room, but not destined to be awarded father of the year. Hunter's mother was as cruel; just less apparent. She was a busy body socialite and only showed an interest in her clubs and committees. Her greatest joy was in front of a camera or reading a write-up about her in a magazine or newspaper article. Hunters status in the family was that of a lampshade; just another fixture in a big house and not much more.

To those on the outside looking in, both the Reynolds and the Worcestershire family seemed to have content and normal lives, but *content* and *normal* was just a camouflage.

* * *

Like Clair, Hunter was also a refugee of sexual abuse. It started when he was five years old. His parents watched over a sixteen-year-old boy who shared a room with him. The memories were so vague that he can't remember his name, or how long he stayed. But whoever it was, Hunter called him Chuck. Years later, he asked his mother who he was, and she didn't have a clue. Hunter thought he was crazy, but remembered what he did to him down to the last detail.

A counselor verified the memory of the event, and said, "Five-year-old kids can't make that shit up."

After Hunter's third time in treatment, he discovered who the abuser was. He did the math, connected the dots, and his parents confirmed it. They knew nothing about a boy named Chuck, but told him an older cousin stayed with them for a few weeks.

"But why the name change?" he asked.

The therapist told him it was a self-defense mechanism. He made up Chuck to disassociate himself from someone he thought was trustworthy and created another to blame —hence, the birth of Chuck. Mystery solved.

Hunter's abuse did not end with "Chuck." At eight years old while on vacation to visit relatives, again the abuse was from older cousins —all brothers in their teens, and lived under the same roof. His folks were always excited to go; after the first trip, Hunter dreaded it.

When they arrived the next year, and after the twelve-hour drive, he stayed at his parent's side as long as he could, which was unprecedented. Even at a young age, he already developed hatred toward his parents, but felt safe when they were around. The sleeping arrangements gave in to the abuse. His parents stayed a few houses down at a friend's place and left Hunter alone with his aunt and cousins. The house was a large two-story home with a game room and three bedrooms on the top floor, a master on the first... with lots of space in between. Hunter was all alone and afraid. Thankfully this was the last evening of the trip.

As usual, right after dinner, his parents prepared for the walk a few houses down to call it an evening. Right as they were about to leave, Hunter ran to his mother and wrapped his arms around her as tight as he could and begged to go with them.

"Now, Hunter, today is our last day here for vacation. You stay here with your cousins so you boys can play together."

He cried uncontrollably, and his mother forced her way out of his grip.

"Hunter, what is wrong with you?"

He staggered backward, with a lowered head and arms straight down at his side.

The elder cousin said, "Yeah, Hunter stay here. We'll play games and have a lot of fun!"

"You see, Hunter? They want you to stay and play. Now you scoot."

After his parents left, Hunter was more frightened than ever and had nowhere to hide, but even if he could— they'd find him, but tonight seemed to start out differently. The four of them watched a movie and Hunter thought maybe they would leave him alone and go to bed afterward. The other boys went to their rooms, and Hunter tried to sleep on the upstairs sofa in the game room. He was sound asleep with the covers pulled over his head, perhaps thinking if he can't see them, they can't see him. Later that night, it started all over again, and it did not differ from before. He pleaded with them to leave him alone.

"Oh, come on, Hunter. It's just good, clean fun."

Hunter's opinion differed. As the hours passed, they handed him around like a little whore from room to room, cousin to cousin. His parents were unaware of what they did to him; he kept it inside and never said a word.

On the way home, everyone was quiet except for some jazz background music playing on the radio.

His mother lowered the volume and asked Hunter, "Wasn't that a nice vacation?"

He stared out the window and said nothing.

"Hunter, your mother asked you a question."

Stoned faced and pale, he said, "I just want to go home."

This went on for three straight summers, and this trip was the last time he ever saw his cousins again.

As a young teen, the sexual abuse stopped, but drugs and alcohol picked up where it left off.

As he got older, those memories haunted him for several years, but he got over it — or so he thought.

Hunter had an older sister, Gail, who also had her fair share of torment; this time, it was their father, but Hunter never knew the specifics. She was four years old, Hunter was three. Most of what he recalled was that she wandered around the neighborhood all the time unattended by either parent. To put an end to it, at least for the short term, their father locked her in her room for several days. They took food to her, but didn't let her use the bathroom, instead, it was a small, plastic training toilet for little kids. In nineteen-sixty, it was rare that the authorities got involved with any child protection, but in this case, they did. A neighbor must have tipped them off. When the social worker arrived, she knocked on the door. There was no answer, and she let herself in.

"Hello. Anyone home?"

She peeked around for a couple of seconds, then Dr. Worcestershire turned the corner and met her a few feet from the door.

"And just who in the hell are you?"

He startled her, but she remained composed.

"Nelda Jones from Social Services."

There were no handshakes during the introduction, only glares.

"Where is your daughter?"

He was acting somewhat anxious and jittery.

"Why is that any of your business?"

Ms. Jones was not as anxious or jittery and got in his face only inches away.

"The protection of children is my business! Now, where is she?"

"I must ask you to leave."

"Oh really? You should look outside. See that man in the fancy uniform and a shiny badge standing next to the pretty vehicle that looks a lot like a police car? Now, doctor, I'll ask again, where is your daughter?"

Dr. Worcestershire opened the blinds enough to peek. The officer noticed him too and gave a condescending two-finger salute.

He closed the blinds and said, "In her room."

"I'd like to see her —now!" He led her down a dark hallway, got to the door and unlocked it. The room was a mess and smelled to high heaven.

"Why is this child locked in this room?"

"To punish her."

"How long do you plan on keeping her here?"

"As long as it takes."

She picked up Gail, holding her with outstretched arms and said, "I have a new plan. You need to wash her and clean up this room."

She handed Gail to the father knowing the feces that covered her would stain his pressed, white shirt.

He clung to her like a sack of potatoes.

"Do you have any idea who I am?" he asked in a condescending tone.

"Yes, I do, and I don't give a damn. I will be back next week, and if I see this again, this child will be removed from this house. Do you understand me?"

He ignored the social workers warning, and when she left, he put Gail down, led her back to the room, tossed a Twinkie on the floor, then locked the door.

The next day, somehow Gail got out, but instead of a stroll around the block, she ran away. Kids are not stupid, they know what love is, and what it isn't, and there wasn't much of it to go around in this household. It was doubtful she had any concept of what running away was, all she knew, even as a child, that this was wrong, and escaped it.

The Worcestershire's owned two German shepherds, who accompanied and protected her as she traveled to a nearby wooded area. The police found Gail playing in a muddy pool of water, and the dogs stood guard and did not let them approach. They notified her father to handle the animals and take her home.

When he arrived, there she was, slapping the water with both hands and making mud-pies. One shepherd sat on the pool's edge next to her, the other animal stared down an officer with his weapon drawn and his target in sight. Dr. Worcestershire whistled to alert the dogs. The dog that sat beside her obeyed the command and jumped in the backseat of the car while the other one was unresponsive and didn't leave her.

Then he shouted, "Rex! Get over here!"

Still nothing. He went to the car, reached in and got a leash. As he approached, Rex growled showing his full set of teeth.

"Don't you growl at me!"

He grabbed him by the snout and shook it violently to let him know who was in charge.

The cop with the gun yelled, "Should I shoot?"

Gail screamed, "*Noooo!*"

She got up and stood between him and the barrel of the gun. Rex released himself from its owner and ran to be with his comrade.

With both animals tucked away in the vehicle, Dr. Worcestershire seized Gail by the arm, spun her around and headed toward the car. His pace was swift, and she had to run to keep up. He threw her in the front seat, thanked the officers and took her home.

Most of what Hunter remembered about his sister were elusive. Gail was removed and placed in foster care regardless of her father's influence. The day the authorities took her away, the mother was emotional, and the father had only two words; good riddance. After they had taken her away, there was a void of time. Several years separated Hunter from his sister, and many memories were lost... except one; a funeral. Gail killed herself at sixteen.

* * *

Coincidence and karma don't seem to be the right words to use in the same sentence; this was the exception. Hunter and Clair were the same age with almost the same timelines of events. Violence, neglect, and abuse were common themes between both families, and Clair and Hunter were collateral damage because of it.

At twenty-eight, they met their suffering head on when it reached its peak. Ten years earlier, the anguish was released, and many years before that, the misery began; the gaps in the middle were a living nightmare. They were amazed they survived and made it this far... at least for now.

Chapter IV

Clair was reading a magazine late in the afternoon. It was four-thirty when the phone rang. She looked at the caller ID and saw it was her mother.

"Oh great."

She hesitated, hoping it would stop ringing and go to her machine, but instead, picked it up.

"Hello, Rae, how are you?"

"Not good. I have some disturbing news."

Clair sat down and acted shocked.

"What is it? Is dad all right?"

"Clair, you know damn well your father is dead."

"Sorry, I keep forgetting. So what is it?"

"Edward is in the hospital."

"Oh my God! What happened?"

Her concerns were exaggerated because she couldn't care less if he was alive or dead; her preference was the latter.

"The high school girls' soccer team got together and beat him up!"

Clair stood and paced as far as the phone cord would go.

"That's terrible!"

She felt her emotions swell and continued pacing. One feeling absent was sympathy.

"You can stop being such a smartass and end the acting."

"You busted me again. I have my serious face on. Please continue."

"Thank God someone pulled them off him and called an ambulance, or lord knows what they would have done. They beat the holy crap out of him. Clair, I'm so upset right now. Please forgive my language. We both know I'm above that kind of filth."

It seemed she was more concerned with her language than Edward's health.

"Run down to the church and say a few Hail Mary's along the way, that will take care of your sin."

"Aren't we the comedian today?"

Clair bit her lip just short of drawing blood. "I'm sorry, I'm as upset as you are."

"You have a helluva way of showing it."

"OK, I'm serious now. Why do you think the girls did it?"

Embarrassed, she replied with a condescending response.

"I believe you and I both know why. A paramedic overheard one girl say they were going to..." then whispered into the phone, "... cut off his dick and toss it in the river."

She got back to her normal speaking voice and continued.

"One of them had already cut through his jeans with a pair of scissors for God's sake!"

Clair couldn't control herself any longer and busted out laughing.

"What's so damn amusing?"

"Sorry again. I saw something funny on the television."

"I didn't think you owned a TV."

She didn't, but improvised.

"It's new. I'll turn it off so we can finish. Be right back."

She took the opportunity and mimicked turning off her imaginary television. Clair covered her mouth and laughed again with the image of Edward getting beaten up by many of the girls he had molested.

"Serves the bastard right."

She gathered her thoughts, composed herself and picked up the phone.

"Now, where were we?"

"The last I recall you were laughing. I also heard you say 'click' when you turned off the TV. I still have mom ears."

"Wow! You heard that?"

Having no care one way or the other, but for her mother's benefit, asked anyway.

"Is he okay?"

"A few cuts and bruises and a gash on the back of his head that needed stitches."

She tried not to laugh again and took a deep breath.

"How long will Edward be in the hospital?"

"Your uncle is there to pick him up."

"Good."

She couldn't hold it back anymore and had to get off the phone before peeing herself.

"I have to go."

Her mother shouted, "Don't you dare hang up the pho—."

She hung up and did bust a gut, then fell to the floor and laughed her ass off.

Clair wished she were at the hospital to finish the job, but thought instead, "*I hope he gets an infection.*"

Those girls taking out years of hostility with each blow to his face brought a smile to her face. The tide had indeed turned. Clair replaced her smile with a somber expression recalling a time when she was little. Edward was six years older than she, and in his prime of abuse toward her. A father of one of the other girls cornered Edward one day and gave him the sternest of warnings.

"You touch my daughter one more time, I will kill you."

He didn't say it figuratively either, he meant —kill him —and Edward knew it.

Taking his advice, Edward left the other girls alone, and Clair became his sole interest for the time being. Stories you've heard on TV or read in the paper, do not compare to the things Edward did to Clair. Most predators will use gentle aggressiveness, kindness, and gifts to develop trust; Edward's was brutal at its core— with no kindness or gifts. Even Frankenstein and The Wolfman had their moments of compassion; never Edward.

It went on for days and often several weeks in a row. During those tortuous days when Clair's parents weren't around, they left her and Edward alone at their house. She was in the third grade; he was in junior high. Many times after school when the parents weren't home, and to delay the inevitable, she'd play at the park or hide at a neighbor's house.

Clair would do this for two or three hours. She'd peek from around a corner to see if the car was in the driveway. When it was, it signaled that the coast was clear, but when it wasn't, she trembled. On many occasions, Clair waited for her parents but knew that sooner or later she had to go home, even when they never showed up. When the time came, took a deep breath and ran as fast as her legs would carry her, then stopped and hid behind a tree or a neighbor's car just long enough to see if Edward was there. Convinced of the possibility he wasn't, ran to the house. Convinced of the possibility he might be, made her hide more. With nothing left to hide behind, she'd make a final sprint to the back door of the house still uncertain of Edwards whereabouts.

During the short jaunt, she'd say to herself over and over again, "Don't be home —don't be home —don't be home. "Her heart would beat so hard, she felt and heard it in her head.

Safely at the door but frightened, Clair tried to sneak in. She'd slowly open the door, and it always creaked a little, when it did, she stopped, listened, then opened it just enough to squeeze by. Looking around one last time, tip-toed through the house and locked herself in her room.

Clair's most frightening moment came on a Friday. Her fears were lessened when Edward was not home, but never diminished. That evening and unknown to her, he was there, lurking in the shadows. Their parents went out with friends and not expected to be back until later that evening; then it began. Locked in her room, Clair heard Edward creeping around the house like some scary monster on the loose. He went from room to room, slamming each door behind him. He knew where she was, but toyed with her anyway.

"Where are you, Clair?"

Then he recited the line from 'hide and seek.' "Ollie ollie oxen free!" he shouted.

"Come out, come out wherever you are."

She sat in the corner beside the bed and clung to her Bible. The footsteps in the distance got louder and louder and stopped, start again, then stop again.

It was eerily silent, and like so many times before, he suddenly and abruptly pounded on the door yelling, "Clair, let me in!"

She tried to cover her ears and block his voice and the noise. Shaking and scared, prayed to God to make him go away. Her prayers were unanswered, and the yelling and pounding continued.

Clair got up and darted to a window and tried to open it and escape, but she was too little to raise it. She ran and placed her back against the door, trying to block his entrance. Her ears were no longer covered and heard his words.

Inches away on the other side of the door, Edward's lips formed a soft, almost gentle smile.

"You scared, little girl?" he asked in a sneering tone.

Edward knew she was against the door and put his face close to it… so close, she felt his breath coming through the crack in the door jamb and had the stench of rotten eggs. He lowered his voice so she could hardly hear.

"The boogeyman is here, and I'm gonna getcha."

Then with a nauseating, guttural tone, he spewed, "Boogga-booggaboogga!"

Clair jumped away and ran to another corner of the room.

This would go on for what seemed an eternity for a little eight-year-old.

She begged and begged for Edward to leave her alone, then yelled, "Go away! Mom and Dad will be home soon!"

At least that was the hope.

Clair knelt on the floor, put her hands together in prayer and bowed her head.

"Please, God, bring Mommy and Daddy home. I'm scared."

Edward glanced at the time and panicked, she looked at her small alarm clock and felt relieved, but the time shortage never stopped him. There would be more yelling and more pounding until there was surrender. To make it end and silence him, she opened the door, then prayed some more.

Although Clair remained silent and told no one —not a soul, her mother eventually found out what Edward had been doing to her. Clair's father was out of town for a few days, and Edward wasn't home, so her mother dealt with the situation alone. Clair was in her bedroom coloring and playing with her toys when she heard someone stomping toward her room and panicked. The door swung wide open, and hit so hard, it banged against the wall leaving a hole.

Her mother stood at the door and shouted.

"Clair Marie! What have you done?"

Clair looked at her with a confused expression. "What is it, Mommy?"

"Get over here, and I mean now!"

Clair placed her crayons back in the box, got off the floor, then stood in front of her mother. She could smell cigarette smoke and vodka coming out of her mouth with every word.

Her mother shook her back and forth, saying, "You are a bad little girl!"

She gazed up at her mother with tears streaming down her face.

"Why am I in trouble? I didn't do anything."

"Shut up!"

She let go, and Clair took two steps back. Her mother crossed her arms and asked, "Did he put 'it' in you?"

Embarrassed and ashamed, she hung her head down.

Crying, she said, "No, Mommy, he 'only' made me touch it," which was a lie; there was a lot more.

From those days forward and when things didn't go as planned, the question of "*what did I do*" always crossed her mind and why she "*deserved it.*" The abuse slowed to a simmer but never stopped. Later on, and in her early teenage years, the physical torment was replaced with verbal threats, teasing, and warnings.

Even in her teenage years, Edward harassed her all the time saying things like, "Someday I will have you," or, "You are all mine and you know it."

Without being too explicit with his coded language, Clair knew what he meant. Those words haunted her for years and took it like a champ — or so she thought.

* * *

It was just another drab evening for Clair, coupled with her scheduled nighttime routine. She picked up where she'd left off the night before, and the night before that, and the night before that. To celebrate her twenty-first birthday, which was a few months ago, treated herself to a casual evening. First stop —McDonald's. She always ordered the kids meal, which included a small cheeseburger, side of fries, diet soda and a toy which added to her collection that could fill a large box. After her feast, it was off to Sid's Bar and Tavern, named after its owner, Charles Sidney. This was her last stop to finish the day until around midnight, then back to her house to polish off the evening with pills and more whiskey.

Clair took her regular seat at the bar, clutched the bottom of the cushion and bounced the stool up and down in short little hop, hop, hops, nudging it forward to move in closer. She straightened her hair, reached into her purse and pulled out a pack of cigarettes.

"What will it be tonight, Clair?"

"I don't know, Charlie."

She tapped the filtered end of the cigarette on the bar and said, "I think I'll mix it up tonight and start with a Scotch soda and a Miller chaser."

Charlie laughed because that was what she always ordered. He turned the bottle over an ice-filled glass and did the "one, two, three" method of pouring. On this night, he went to four, then topped it with a splash of soda.

"Why, thank you, Charlie. Feeling charitable this evening?"

He handed her the drink then wiped the bar clean with a fresh towel.

"You looked like you needed a stiff drink. Rough day at the office?"

She downed her drink in two quick single gulps, chomped on a piece of ice while Charlie slid a bottle of Miller down the bar like a hockey puck aiming for its target; Clair's awaiting grasp. It was poetry in motion; they'd had a lot of practice.

After some time, she tipped the bottle and guzzled the last few drops of the barley and hops nectar then motioned with her spent bottle that signaled another round. Charlie got a clean glass, emptied a scoop of ice, and poured.

"Charlie, this time, hold the soda and make it a double."

He complied, then sat the glass in front of her, grabbed another towel and wiped it again.

He stopped with the wiping, looked at her, and in a concerned tone, asked, "What's on your mind, Clair? You don't seem to be your regular, jovial self."

She placed both elbows on the counter, one hand on her chin and the other balancing her drink.

"Charlie, I can't get motivated anymore. I go to my studio every morning and stare at a blank canvas —all day long."

"Boy trouble?"

"Sort of."

"Let me guess —Hunter?"

She sighed and replied, "Who else? Yes, we broke up again."

"Why don't you take up knitting? That doesn't take much thinking, just go 'knit and curl.'"

Bartenders are great at giving advice, and she chuckled a little.

"Amusing, Charlie. I don't think that's a knitting term."

He replied, "How would I know? I don't knit."

"Oh, that old excuse," then Clair let out a whispered snicker and chugged the rest of her drink.

"Charlie, I'm taking off. It's getting close to midnight."

He wiped the counter again, and she told him he was going to wear a hole in the bar, then he chuckled.

"Good night. You have yourself a safe evening and be careful out there. Don't worry about Hunter. He'll be back around," he said as he continued wiping.

"That's what I'm afraid of. I'll see you tomorrow night."

"I don't think so."

"Why?"

"Because today is Wednesday and you don't do Thursdays. Remember?"

"Oh yeah. I guess I'll see you Friday."

This was her schedule every night except for Sunday and Thursday. Thursday was her day to rest up for Friday night's festivities and left Sunday open to attend a church service... usually with a hangover. She always went with the intentions of cleansing her soul, but in her mind, there was none to cleanse and believed hers was lost years ago. The things she felt responsible for could never be forgiven and going to church was more of a habit than a desire for inner peace and tranquility; besides, it had been an excuse to see Hunter, her on-again, off-again boyfriend. He went for much the same reason. It was also his excuse to see his on-again, off-again girlfriend, Clair.

Chapter V

A year later, Clair slowed down on the pills and booze, but never to a full halt.

Her reasoning was unclear for the sudden shift, but thought, "*Nothing else is working. What could it hurt?*"

A friend introduced her to AA and took her to some meetings. To her, it was the dumbest thing in the world, but went along just to shut up her friend.

The few meetings Clair attended, she fidgeted in the chair, played with her hair and mocked its members in her mind.

"*Hi, my name is so and so, and I'm an alcoholic.*"

Then the typical response.

"*Hi, so and so! Glad you're here!*"

Her thoughts continued as she played along, only this time, stood up and told them aloud.

"Hi, my name is Clair, and you people are a bunch of idiots!"

There were no chants of, "Hi, Clair," only silence from a beleaguered crowd and many stares.

"Big deal. I'm out of here."

And she did. Clair got to her feet and left.

She never attended another meeting and had proven to herself she could go at it alone.

Clair was cautioned that quitting on her own was not a good idea. Her friend insisted she needed support from other members of the group.

"Hey, I've already slowed down on everything, and I did it all by myself."

Then her friend asked, "But have you stopped?"

"I'm getting there."

About a week later, she took inventory of the pills and booze and noticed a difference.

"This is great!"

There was more of each than expected.

"This is really working. I'm saving a bundle!"

Though she continued down the same road as before, but reasoned she could handle it this time.

"I will not be a slave to either of you again," then made herself a drink.

She was proud she rarely got drunk anymore, at least not stumbling drunk. Clair explained it away in her own words, that "*she only caught a buzz*," but those buzzes were an everyday thing.

Clair didn't live far from the bar and walked both ways. After finishing the evening and during her stroll back to her apartment, she would stop and gaze at the billboards along the way to see if any of them had changed. This fixation went on for months.

One evening, perhaps for the hundredth time, stared up at one of them, but this time, threw her hands in the air and said aloud, "What the hell am I going to do with my life?"

Then, like a crazy lady, screamed at the top of her lungs, "When are you going to change the fucking sign?"

Clair made it home, got to the door, pulled out her keys and let herself in. She flipped on the entryway light, then heard a loud pop and a simultaneous flash, like an old Kodak camera.

"Dammit to hell! Why now?"

She tossed a leftover bag of fries on the floor and felt her way down the small enclosed hallway that led to the bedroom. Both arms were outstretched and flailed them around in the darkness like a blind person. She got to her room and sat on the edge of the bed, then reached over to turn on the lamp. It had three brightness settings: high, medium, or low — and chose the latter. With a few turns of the button and two clicks later… wha-la! Though the light was on low, it was enough to illuminate pill bottles, an empty fifth of whiskey, and one unopened bottle of Vodka, all of which occupied the nightstand.

Things in Clair's mind continued to haunt her… like wanting to die. After years of demons chasing around in her head, including the recent breakup with Hunter… again, were enough of an excuse to take matters on her own. That day was her twenty-second birthday, but on this occasion, it wasn't months ago… it was today.

Clair sat there for over an hour, and contemplated her life, questioning what it all meant and concluded at that moment — *"Not much."*

She got to her feet with determined resolve and announced to herself, "I didn't have a say-so about coming into the world, but by God, I can decide how I go out."

Clair took a deep breath and decided tonight was the night. With just enough light, she tip-toed toward the kitchen, and not sure why the need to tip-toe; she was alone. Perhaps it was just an old habit.

She turned on the light above the sink and opened a drawer.

"Oops! Wrong one."

It was the infamous junk drawer and slid open the next one. It squeaked and rattled all the way out, then rummaged through it and selected a knife.

Clair examined it.

"Damn, I cut up a chicken with this the other day. What would the chicken think?"

She giggled at her own silly joke, then wept.

It was a broad-bladed butcher knife that had a polished, mirror-like finish. Clair held the knife at eye level. With a stoic and curious expression on her face, flipped it up and down with little movement, as if focusing it. She stood there in silence and stared at the distorted, reflected image of herself.

Clair had made several attempts in the past to kill herself, but this time had a look of determination and an uneasy feeling this might be the end. She went back to the bedroom and turned the lamp up a notch for better lighting. While she was at it, went through her pre-printed to do list, with a check box beside each task and went down the list line-by-line.

"Pay bills...," and marked it.

"I don't want bad credit. Hairdresser... check. I have to look nice."

The next one always tickled her.

"Gas?"

She always read it as a question and commented out loud, "Nope, feeling pretty good."

Last on the list —the grocery store.

Clair studied it for a moment, and instead of a check mark, she crossed it off.

"I won't be needing any."

She glanced over the list one more time, tore off the page and threw it in the trash.

"I'm sick and tired of being pushed around and told what to do, especially by a piece of paper. Tonight, it will be a *to-did* list."

She tossed the rest of the unused pad with the other piece of paper.

Clair researched the usual ways of killing yourself.

"Pills? Too Marilyn Monroe-ish. Besides, they are to be used with whiskey to relax. On the other hand, they were good enough for her, so they should be good enough for me. But with my luck, I'd get sick and puke them out. What a waste."

She was obsessed with the pills, read the warning label and took inventory.

"And what if I succeed?"

The thought of being hauled out naked on a stretcher was too humiliating and mumbled, "I just couldn't live with myself."

Then asked herself out loud in a higher octave, "I just couldn't live with myself?"

She shook her head and said, "What an idiot."

Clair rattled the pill bottle once more and tossed it on the bed concluding that pills were too chancy and wasn't risking it. More ideas came to her, then snapped her fingers.

"I've got it! Jump from a building?"

Then paused, "No, too dramatic; besides, I'm afraid of heights. Pistol? Gross!"

She worried she'd wound herself enough to put her in a permanent coma.

"Now that's really depressing," then said aloud, "I sure as hell wouldn't want to inconvenience anyone, sort of defeats the purpose."

Clair continued the conversation with herself.

"Hanging? *Hmmm*, now there's an option. But knowing some of my idiot friends like I do, I'm sure one of them would say something stupid at the funeral like, *That Clair, what a swinger.* So, hanging's out."

Clair came across a book about four years earlier about how to kill yourself. At the time of the purchase, she was certain it didn't get on a bestseller list.

Her next thought was, "*What kind of sicko would write such a thing?*"

She picked it up at a local used bookstore and wondered if the previous owner used its advice. And for a second, it creeped her out.

She'd never read it that hard before, but tonight felt the need to study it and pay attention to details. After a few minutes, and several scanned pages later, concluded that one of the best ways to off yourself was by slashing the wrists. According to the book, with the success of a lethal cut, it was relatively painless… "like dying in slow motion."

"I guess I'm on to something," then picked up the blade and mimicked a line in a marriage ceremony.

"With this knife, I do thee die."

Taking a deep breath, lowered the blade and did a small cut to her arm, but decided it wasn't sharp enough. She relaxed for a moment to re-group and contemplated her next move. Clair did not want to become a victim of hesitation wounds. Hesitation wounds are what they imply; for people too chicken to follow through with a lethal cut, just a bunch of little ones. They might get lucky and cut through a decent bleeder, but it takes a while. Oh sure, they'll carry out the mission sooner or later, but it's a lot of wasted time, energy, and unnecessary pain to get the desired result. She popped another pill and took a shot of whiskey.

"If I'm going to do this, let's get it right."

Clair tossed the knife on the floor, went to the art studio attached to her apartment, and found an X-acto blade.

"This should do the trick."

She ran back to her room and picked up the handbook to revisit some of its pages, flipping to the part that tells how to cut yourself.

Clair glanced at its illustrations and directions then said aloud, "Oh my God! I've been doing it wrong the whole time."

Now she knew the Hollywood style of slitting your wrist wasn't enough, referring to those little slices across the wrist. It also recommended doing it in a bathtub; it's easier for others to clean up the mess. Clair had little concern about tidiness, so the bedroom would be just fine.

To do it right, you take the tip of the razor on your forearm, somewhere between the wrist and your elbow. With the blade facing your palm, slice down along the vein towards the wrist.

"Now, I need the guts to do it. Maybe I should use a magic marker and plot the course to be on the safe side. Surgeons do it, so why shouldn't I?"

She jumped up again, ran back to the studio, opened two or three drawers and found a black, fine-tipped marker. Clair slammed the drawer and hurried back to her bedroom and made several more trips; wrong size blade or not the right marker. Her breathing got heavier and heavier after all the running back and forth, then collapsed in her chair.

"The hell with killing myself; I'm going to die from exhaustion!"

She relaxed for a few more minutes, popped one more pill and took another swig.

"Oh shit! I forgot to leave the notes!"

Clair ran back to the kitchen, reached into the junk drawer and pulled out a yellow sticky pad.

"Oh, great, more pads."

She removed three and wrote the words. The first was to her mother.

"Have a nice day," then the next one, "Dear Hunter, I hope you have a good life."

And finally, "My dearest Charlie, I'm sorry I had to do this. Your friend, Clair."

After they had been written, she stuck them to the wall.

Clair got back to the task at hand, settled in, took the marker and charted its path down her arm as instructed. Disappointed with the markings, she ran to the bathroom and scrubbed her arms clean.

"And I call myself an artist."

Clair dried her arm, went to her room again, sat down, and repeated the same procedure as before, this time with more attention to detail.

When finished with the marker, she tossed it aside. "Much better. Cleaner lines."

Afterward, she picked up the blade and turned it toward her skin.

"Here we go."

She chose a starting point, pressed the blade against her skin and moved it slowly down her forearm. Clair was nervous, but more unsteady, and skipped parts of her arm as it traveled a few centimeters that only resulted with a few slight cuts.

"Not enough blood."

She wasn't fully committed to the task at hand and had only grazed herself.

"Dammit, I get more blood when I shave my fucking legs!"

She sat the knife on the edge of the nightstand and knocked over the open bottle of pills.

"My damn luck," then knelt on the floor, swept the pills into her hand like a dustpan, and placed them back in the bottle.

"What is it going to take to finish the job? More pills? More whiskey? Bigger, sharper knife? God only knows. This suffering will end by my hand —tonight."

The biggest concern Clair had with killing herself, was most think if you are an artist like her, that's the way they do it.

"It would be a lot easier if a dump truck would come along and squash me!"

She continued with her delusional imagery.

"*I can see it now; the church is melancholy. Soft organ music is echoing in the background playing 'Amazing Grace' and a flower-covered casket lies in state, front and center, and a crowd of twenty on the back two rows.*"

She paused for a moment and imagined overhearing a conversation between two old church ladies at the funeral.

"*She was so young. Why did she do it?*"

The other whispered, "*Because she was an artist.*"

More of her thoughts continued.

"*See what I mean? The usual bunch are shedding a few tears and still asking why? Because the old lady is right! I'm a fucking artist, that's why! Moron.*"

With yet another failed attempt to end her life, said again to herself, "This will have to wait until another time. I'm too tired."

All that was left to do for the evening was to remove the notes from the wall and set them aside.

Clair reached for the blade one last time, turned it side-to-side, and tried to catch another image of herself on the tiny blade. All it had were smears of blood. She wiped it clean with her shirt and laid it on the nightstand, then crawled into bed, turned off the light and covered herself with a quilt her grandmother made when she was a baby. Clair bunched up a small corner of the quilt, held it to her face, and gave it a whiff.

Drunk and high from the pills, plus a little pain from the cuts, she said "I miss you, Granna," then cried herself to sleep.

* * *

Clair cursed each new day, but on this one, it was worse. She crawled out of bed, put on her slippers and stepped on a few capsules and pills strewn on the floor from the night before. The hardened, jellied ones beneath her feet crunched like a cockroach that just met its fate. She gathered the powdered remains of the pills and broken capsules, then placed them in a cup.

"I'll save this for a late-night cocktail. Waste not, want not."

Besides destroying some of her pharmaceuticals and nursing a hangover, her day started with the same monotony as everyone else, except Clair's; hers included a shower to clean her blood-encrusted arms. She stood naked in front of the bathroom mirror, held up her arms and rotated them back and forth to get a clear view of the damage.

"I can't be seen like this. No need scaring the neighbors."

She lowered them and turned toward the shower a few steps away and said to herself, "Who'd want to live next to a suicidal maniac like me?"

Then she stared back at the mirror.

"Suicide?"

Although she has tried many times before, Clair had never said that word, at least not to refer to her own efforts at suicide, instead, she'd use encrypted language like, "I want to end it all," or, "I don't want to go on anymore," and others. Putting a label on it gave her a moment of pause, but little concern, however, it was still a revelation of sorts.

"I'm glad I got that out of the way. I'm not in denial anymore. And yes, I know… it isn't a river in Egypt. Those AA bastards would be proud."

Clair stumbled her way to the shower and rinsed her wounds. She watched the river of fresh blood combined with the remains of reconstituted scabs flow down the drain. With the shower complete, she dried off, then saw traces of blood stains and splatters all over the towel in blotches.

"Damn! I need to buy red ones from now on."

She tossed it in the corner with the others, threw on a robe and went toward the kitchen and poured a cup of coffee.

"Thank God I wasn't too drunk to set the timer."

Clair staggered back to her bedroom, plopped down on the chair, stirred in six cubes of sugar and tried to sober up. Pills were still scattered all over the place, and the full, unopened bottle of vodka the day before was half-empty.

Chapter VI

Two years earlier, Clair's mother had her committed after another failed suicide attempt; a court order got Hunter there. They were patients at a psych and substance abuse hospital. This was their first go at treatment, and both were diagnosed with depression and a variety of other disorders that also included drug and alcohol abuse.

Their first encounter was a few days after they were admitted, and it was then the two were first introduced. Most of the clients were in the day room, a few others visited in the lounge area sharing idle chat; Hunter and Clair were two of the participants. Like the gentleman he could sometimes be, stood up, walked toward her and removed his ball cap.

He extended his hand and introduced himself.

"Hi, my name is Hunter, and yours?"

She stayed seated and clasped his, then like an innocent southern belle replied, "Nice to make your acquaintance, kind sir. I'm Clair."

"The pleasure is all mine, young miss."

He returned his cap to its well-worn resting place and plopped down on a chair.

The next thing Hunter said to Clair was, "We hardly know each other, and we already have something in common."

She picked at her nails and asked, "And what would that be?"

He stood up and announced, "We're both down in the dump drug addicts."

She thought it was funny; it even made her laugh, which was rare in those days, but took a moment and corrected him.

"I'm not a drug addict; I only do pills and alcohol. That other stuff will kill you."

Now he laughed.

"What's so funny?" she asked.

"My mother only does pills too, and I guarantee, she needs to be here worse than I do."

Clair giggled, "Mine too. By the way, how do you know so much stuff about me?"

"I read your chart."

"You what?" she exclaimed.

Hunter changed the subject.

"You know this isn't the first time we've met."

"Really? Where?"

"At Sid's a few months ago,"—then whispered, "I have a fake ID."

Already bored with him and the conversation, Clair sat in a slumped position still picking her fingernails.

"Big deal, I have one too, ever since I was fifteen."

By now, she was getting annoyed and asked, "Excuse me, I know your name, but who are you?"

"Oh, come on, I was the guy that said 'hi' at Sid's."

She laughed out loud, "Oh, yeah," and continued with a hint of sarcasm, "and you think you're the only guy who ever said 'hi' to me."

"You were alone, and I sat beside you at the bar and asked why you were there."

Her laughing stopped, then sat up and took a serious look at him.

"I remember you."

"Do you recall what you said?"

Clair paused for a moment.

"Yes, I do."

She stared away from him and tried to recall the conversation, and she did.

"I said I had nowhere else to be."

Hunter reached out and touched her shoulder.

"You're right. It was sad then, and hearing you say it again, it's still sad. Have things gotten any better?"

Clair let out a subdued 'ha.'

"Depends on how you define better. I'm still here, aren't I?"

Clair and Hunter experienced the worst of the worst, and only occasionally the best of the best. They had a happy childhood if infancy counts. All the history after that was a living hell, but they endured and tried to have a normal life, whatever normal looked like.

* * *

Clair's relationship with Hunter ended almost as soon as it began. It's hard enough for sane people to make it in this world, but they met under unusual circumstances. They were a couple and broke up and got back together more times than you can count. How could they not? They seemed to care for each other, and a year later tried living together. It didn't work out. He moved in one weekend and was out the next.

Clair had a busy schedule and several errands that would take most of the day. She got an early start, and Hunter stayed in bed.

He sat up, put a pillow behind him, and asked, "How long will you be gone?"

"I'll be back around four or five," she said while gathering a few things shoving them into a briefcase.

Grinning, he said, "That's a long time. I'll whip up something to eat before you get back."

"Stouffer's lasagna?"

"Only the finest for you, my sweet."

Clair was impressed he could operate a microwave.

Her first order of business was to find a new hairdresser. She visited one of her friends who "played on the other side of the fence" and asked if he knew any gay hairdressers because she thought they were the best.

He jotted down a few names on a napkin and handed it to her.

"That's a short list," she said while scanning it.

"I made it easy. Those are the ones who aren't."

An hour later, Clair realized she'd forgotten paperwork that needed to be signed back at the apartment. When she arrived, heard moaning coming from her bedroom and sneaked down the hall toward it. Using her pinkie finger, nudged the cracked opened door to get a peek. She said nothing at first and only stared. She tilted her head a little to get a better view of the movements. Like watching a tennis match, her head went back and forth with each gyration.

Then thought, "*I didn't know a human body could bend like that.*"

Clair's emotions went from curious to pissed and kicked the door wide-open.

The girl yelled, "Oh fuck!"

"I agree, that appears to be what's going on."

The girl moved away from Hunter and covered herself.

"You don't have to be so shy, sweetie; I already saw your ass."

Hunter had panic in his voice because of his current set of circumstances. He searched his entire vocabulary for what to say.

"Clair, I know what you're thinking, and it's not what it looks like."

"You know what, Hunter? I was born at night, not last night."

During this exchange of words, they heard the front door slam. Somehow Hunter's "friend" got dressed, slipped out of the bedroom, ran down the hallway and escaped.

"Why didn't you ask her to stay for dinner?" Clair asked.

"I would have, but you chased her off."

That was his effort to lighten the mood, but it wasn't working.

"I'm not amused."

He got out of bed and draped a blanket around his naked body. He approached Clair, and when he got close, she slapped the hell out of him.

"Why did you hit me?"

"That was a slap, Hunter."

Then she doubled her fist and punched him in the stomach, not very hard, but to illuminate the difference.

"That was a hit."

Hunter recovered from both. He hardly felt the punch to the gut; the slap was a different story. He rubbed his red and swelling face to ease the discomfort.

"Clair, it was nothing."

"From where I was standing, it didn't look like nothing."

"You know what I mean," he said while trying to recover, but she wasn't buying it.

"Yeah, I know what you mean. Hell, I was about to take notes!"

Then thought, "*I need to exercise a lot more, with emphasis on the stretchy ones.*"

She looked at her watch, tapped it twice and said, "I need for you to gather yourself and your shit and get out."

"Are you serious?"

"Look at me, Hunter, do I look serious?"

He packed his things right away, and while he did, she shouted from the other side of the apartment, "I'll have to burn the blanket and sheets —maybe the whole damn bed! Asshole!"

He took five minutes to collect his things; he was a light packer. They met at the front door which Clair opened and motioned for him to leave, followed by a single foot stomp on the floor.

"Now, get out!"

Stepping out, he turned to her and said, "I guess I screwed up."

"You guessed right. Was that girl one of your groupies?"

Hunter nervously laughed while she waited for an answer.

"Not that one."

His response got her attention. By now, anger turned livid. She leaned against the threshold with arms crossed.

"That one? Are there others?"

"Not anymore. You will get a hoot out of this when I tell you. I met her at your art exhibit last month."

Clair replied, "I'm glad one of us got something out of it."

* * *

Even after she tossed him out, they still tried to put the broken pieces of their relationship back together. It didn't work out so good for Humpty Dumpty, so how could it for them? For months, their fragile relationship unraveled even further, and doom was its destiny.

While together and not arguing over something stupid, they got along great. Both seemed to have a knack for starting a fight like what movie to see or where to eat —and other times it was something else... like this.

Clair had been running around town for art supplies and some groceries. Later, she stopped and visited with friends. After a few hours of mindless conversation, decided it was time to go home. After the thirty-minute drive back to her apartment, the couch looked inviting.

Exhausted, she sprawled out on it, flipping around trying to find the perfect position to get comfortable. She fluffed one of its cushions to rest her head and nodded off. The phone rang, and it startled her, then rolled over and fell off the couch— banging her big toe on the coffee table on the way down.

"Ouch! Someone will pay for this!"

She didn't bother getting up and crawled to the phone. The caller ID was from "unknown," but picked it up anyway.

"Hello! Who in the hell is this?"

"Hi Clair, it's me."

She yawned, stretched, and guessed, "Hunter?"

"Yeah, it's me. How's it going?"

"I'm all right," Then a little irritated, added, "until the damn phone rang. It's after midnight!"

"Sorry bout' that."

"You should be. I thought you were coming over tonight —I meant last night. Shit! I can't think straight. Yesterday!"

Hunter was doing his best thinking on his feet.

"I would have, but I got distracted."

She picked herself off the floor and sat down on the couch.

"Distracted? How?"

He seemed a little nervous, and just spit it out.

"It's hard to explain. Here's the short version —I'm in jail."

"Yeah, I'd call it a distraction. What did you do this time?"

"It started out innocent enough..."

"I'm sure it did."

"May I finish? Me and a few buddies went to a bar over at the west end, and..."

"And what?"

"We were having a big ole' time minding our own business, and..."

She crossed her arms.

"I'm listening," though with not much enthusiasm.

"I got busted for public intoxication."

"They don't usually throw you in jail for a PI if you have a ride."

"There's more."

Now she's getting pissed.

"Of course there is."

"I got into a scuffle with some dude."

"Just a scuffle? Again, they don't throw you in jail because of a little fight."

"They do when you hit a cop."

"You what?" she exclaimed. "You hit a cop, end up in jail, and you call that a distraction?"

"Semantics, Clair. It sounds worse than it is. You see, the cop was separating us, a fist flew — that would be mine — and he got in between me and the other guy's face."

"Semantics, my ass! You're in some deep shit this time."

"Don't worry, there's a happy ending... sort of."

"I can't wait to hear this."

"They aren't charging me with assaulting a cop, just the PI. He was cool and knew I didn't mean to hit him; besides, it was just a tap... I think. Can you bail me out? I've been in here all night long."

"You're breaking my heart. I should let your ass stay in jail. You still owe me from the last time."

Then he begged, "Please, Clair, I promise this will be the last time, and don't tell my parents."

His promise fell on deaf ears.

"That's what you said the last time and the time before that."

"But this time, I mean it."

Then she repeated herself.

"That's what you said the last time and the time before that."

"OK, Clair. I get it! I heard it the first time!"

He was already frustrated, and now he was the one getting angry being reminded of the truth.

"Could you please give me a fucking break?"

Her anger peaks his.

"You don't listen, Hunter! Why can't we do things like a normal couple, and no, I won't tell your parents. I don't even know them. That would be an awkward conversation, now wouldn't it? Hi, my name is Clair. We don't know each other, but I have been dating your son for a while, and wanted to let you know that he's in jail."

Hunter agreed.

"I guess you're right. Not a very good introduction," then came the bartering.

"Come and get me and we'll go on a date."

"Yeah, to fill out paperwork at the bail bondsman's office. That's what a girlfriend does all the time —spend an evening at the police station bailing out their idiot boyfriend!"

"Will you?"

She hesitated and agreed, but thought to herself, "*Who's more of a fool? Him for getting tossed in jail or me getting him out?*"

Laughing a little, Hunter said, "At least we'll be together."

Again, more thoughts to herself, "*Not for long.*"

She got dressed and microwaved a cup of old tea.

"The little bastard can wait," then threw on a scarf, wrapped it around her neck, and aimed out the door. She was not in a big hurry to get to the police station and took the scenic route which added an extra thirty minutes. When Clair arrived, Hunter was in the lobby waiting.

"How did you get out?"

"Oh, I forgot to mention it. It's a new day —bondsmen make house calls. I filled out a form, gave them two or three references—" then he leaned in close to her and whispered, "I used your father as one of them. Kinda funny, huh?"

"Hilarious."

He stood and pronounced, "And here we are. Let's get away from this place and go to your apartment."

"My apartment? What for?"

He grabbed Clair with one arm and drew her close. With foul breath and a mischievous grin, said, "You know."

"Know what? If you're thinking what I think you're thinking, you are out of your mind!"

She struggled to free herself, then said, "I'm not in much of a mood to fix you a sandwich, much less anything else."

"Fine with me. Can you give me a ride and loan me a hundred bucks? I have to drop the cash off at the bondsman's office."

"Let me get this straight. So far, I'm just a ride, your banker, and a screw. How close am I?"

"When you put it that way it doesn't sound too good."

"Get your sorry ass in the car before I change my mind."

* * *

Hunter and Clair were two lost souls, and for whatever reason, radiated toward one another. It would be romantic to suggest they found each other like two ships lost at sea, but with these two, it was more like the Titanic running into an iceberg.

A week after Hunter's brief incarceration, his parents were away for the weekend and had the house to himself and was preparing dinner. On the rare occasion he did something sweet and thoughtful, this was his way of thanking and apologizing for what he had put her through after getting thrown in jail — and Clair showed up drunk, which was not unusual and getting worse.

She was primed and ready to go out for a night on the town. All he wanted was for her to let go of her brain for an evening, have a meal, enjoy herself and skip the bar. But no, she had to invite her mother and brother along, and the bloodbath started right away. This was not Hunter's "first rodeo" and knows better than to argue with Clair in her current state. Drunk logic and behavior know no bounds.

The ship set sail, and Clair was the one who tossed in the iceberg.

Clair took a cab, and when she got there, Hunter met her at the door. She stumbled through the doorway and tripped over a rug. Hunter helped get her off the floor.

"Are you okay?"

She didn't answer. He led the way to the kitchen, and she leaned against the countertop to keep herself propped up. Hunter went to the stove, then Clair crossed her arms, and this is how it begins.

"I want to ask you a question."

Hunter thought, "*Oh boy, here we go*," then asked, "What?"

Clair moved away from the countertop, staggered around and slurred her words, then uttered, "I hate my mother and brother."

Hunter was busy with his sauce and said, "Clair, that isn't a question."

"Don't start with me, Hunter!"

He turned toward her, and said, "Start what? You're drunk!"

"No, I'm not. I'm tired."

He grabbed her arm.

"I'm tired too, but you don't see me about to collapse, do you?"

"Let go of my arm! You're an idiot!"

She wiggled free, and he said, "One night, Clair, can it just be you and me for one damn night and leave your family out of it?"

"How can I? They are destroying my life! Now get me a drink!"

Hunter ignored the request and returned to the meal planning. While he was busy tossing a salad, she rummaged through the cupboard to find something to drink.

With his back still turned, asked, "How are they destroying your life?" then said, "They're nowhere to be seen. It's only you and me."

Clair's only response was a continued rant.

"I know what they want."

"What?"

With slurred language and sputtered speech, she said, "They want to destroy me! That's what. Are you stupid?"

"I get it. How many times do you need to repeat it?" he said in a sarcastic tone.

He didn't look at her and continued to cook.

"Clair, you are not that important. Why would they want to destroy you?"

"They want me to be just like them."

"What in the hell are you talking about? How is destroying you going to make you be like them?"

She staggered about still looking for something to drink, and said, "You're not my fucking therapist!"

Clair continued slamming one door then opening the next.

"What are you looking for?"

"None of your damn business."

The last cupboard she visited, had his mother's fine crystal placed in rows like little soldiers. Clair scooted them aside looking for a spot where some booze might be hiding. As she did, a long-stemmed wine glass came crashing down on the counter top, then continued its journey to the floor and broke into a thousand pieces.

In a panic, Hunter turned and yelled, "Holy shit! My mother is going to kill me!"

She disregarded the disaster as Hunter knelt to the floor and cleaned up the shattered remains. As he picked up the pieces, Clair noticed a shard of the broken crystal on the counter-top. She examined its size and sharp edges. It was a small piece in the shape of a dagger that measured about three-inches long. She held it up to the light and admired the rainbow colors that illuminated from it, then lowered it to her hand and slowly made a deep gash along the crease of her palm. The cut went from one side to the other. There was no blood at first, just an open wound. Seconds later, it flowed. Clair felt the warmth of the blood and gazed in amazement at the small puddle of the precious fluid. She cupped her hand, and the once small puddle became a lake.

Hunter was still busy and not a witness to what she did to herself. Some of the blood leaked through her fingers, then the dam burst. It hit the floor and splattered everywhere... reminiscent of a crime scene photo.

Hunter jumped to his feet and exclaimed, "What in the hell are you doing, Clair?"

He took the piece of glass away from her and tossed it with the others, then got a clean towel.

"What am I going to do with you?" he said while wrapping her hand.

Hunter held the towel tight enough to stop the bleeding. Within a minute or two, the rag was soaked and heavy with her blood. He removed it long enough to make a quick examination, then re-wrapped it.

"You've really made a mess of yourself."

While she staggered, said, "It's just a scratch."

With his other hand, Hunter grabbed her.

"Scratch, my ass! This is going to need several stitches."

In a drunk, condescending tone, she mumbled, "You're not a doctor."

"You are right, Clair, I'm not."

Again, ignoring him, jerked herself away and asked, "Do you have anything to drink, or must a girl thirst to death?"

"You have got to be kidding! You've had plenty. Sit down and let me clean you up, then somewhere along the way finish dinner."

Clair tripped over her own feet and fell back hitting against the counter.

"The hell with dinner! You don't understand. How could you?"

Hunter turned away from her and went toward the trashcan, then she grabbed his arm and spun him around, smearing blood all over his arm. She could barely stand and wobbled uncontrollably.

"You are not listening to me!"

She used a shaking finger and aimed it at his face pointing it back and forth with each word, then said, "They... want... to... destroy... me!"

"Clair, you are crazy. You are destroying yourself with shit like this!" he said while waving the rag in her face.

"Whatever you paid your counselor and the rest of those morons was too much. You need a refund."

"Go to hell!"

"You go to hell! They need to lock you up somewhere and throw away the key. I'm sick of this shit! You keep letting your family occupy your mind rent free, and I'm the one who keeps paying for it. You need serious help."

She shouted, "Fuck you!"

"Fuck you!" he shouted louder.

"All I wanted to do was fix a meal, and you had to ruin it!"

Not the most mature thing to do, but Hunter shoved the whole meal down the disposal and tossed everything else into the trashcan.

"There went twenty dollars' worth of shrimp and pasta. I hope you're happy."

Ignoring him again, asked, "Where's my drink?"

"That's it! Go to my room, and I'll clean everything up."

"I'm not staying with you... you... you fucking loser. You're just like them."

Hunter threw his arms in the air in frustration.

"How, Clair? How am I like them?"

"Because you take up for those bastards."

"How can I? I don't even know them."

"That doesn't matter, you are, and you know it."

"Please, Clair, go pass out somewhere and leave me alone. I've learned my lesson."

"And what is that?"

"Don't do anything nice for a psychopath."

"See! See what I mean? You are just like them. You want to destroy me too."

"Clair, I know I've done a lot of rotten things, and I'm trying to get better, but you fight me all the way. Why can't we have one night together without bringing your family along? You were dealt a shitty hand, and I'm sorry, but you are not the only one who hurts. I hurt too, all the time. But sometimes, even for a moment, let that shit go."

"I wish I could, but I can't," she said with a tone of surrender then fell to the floor.

"You've said it a thousand times, it's just a decision away, and now you need to decide. This is getting old."

She looked up at him from the floor and asked, "So, are you done with me too?"

Hunter went to the door, then turned toward her.

"I love you, Clair, but I don't know how much more of this I can take."

She cradled her face with both palms, including the bloody one, and sobbed.

"Love? I don't understand love; it's just a word in the dictionary."

Frustrated and angry, Hunter pounded his head with his fist as hard as he could. With blood covering her face, she crawled over to him and grabbed his leg.

"Stop it! Why are you hitting yourself?"

He stopped with the hitting long enough to respond. Hunter knelt down to her eye level and just a couple of inches from her face, then yelled, "To keep from beating the hell out of you! Go to bed! I can't do this anymore! All I wanted was to have dinner, and all you can do is fight and argue."

He got back to his feet and continued.

"You can't settle for only fanning the flame, you have to pour gas on it."

"So, it's my fault?"

"This time, yes, it is."

"So, I am just like them?"

"My guess is, yes —yes you are just like them."

Clair got herself off the floor, lunged at Hunter and tried to hit him.

"No, I'm not! I'm nothing like them!"

During the attack, he held back both of her hands protecting himself. He pushed her away then she stumbled, fell back to the floor and cried. Then came more, out of sync conversation.

"You don't know what it's like to have your brother rub his dick all over your face and unload his stuff all over you."

"You're right, Clair. Mine were cousins."

"Yeah, but did they ever...?"

This back and forth exchange of 'who had it worse,' would go on for what seemed an eternity. Hunter tried to end the conversation and threw his hands in the air.

"Clair, you win."

"Win what?" she said while getting to her feet.

"You have it shittier than anyone on the planet. You win the grand prize. I give up."

Hunter decided he needed a smoke and some fresh air. He was about to leave but had one more thing to say.

"Clair, maybe you should be like your family, it sure as hell can't be any worse than this."

To the point of almost passing out, she said, "When they own you as a kid; they own you as an adult."

Hunter responded, "Not if you don't let them."

"Well, they do," then she slumped back to the floor and fell asleep.

Events like these were never few and far between. The history they brought into each other's lives, confrontations like these were commonplace; this was one of many.

She woke up the next morning with the mother of all hangovers, and not too sure how she wound up at her apartment. Her first challenge was to get out of her pull-over shirt with a mass of vomit all over it. She thought it would be better to cut the damn thing off rather than pulling it over her head. Hunter stayed the night but had already left for work. Topless and shaky, she poured herself a bowl of cereal and attempted to put the events of the past evening into context and came up short, then glanced at her stitched-up hand. She marveled at the needle work. Hunter did take her to the hospital, and because she was passed out and limp, he saved a bundle on anesthetic medication.

Last night, this morning and the afternoon were now in the past, and the nightlife was right around the corner.

Chapter VII

"Fake it til you make it" was the unofficial motto at the psych hospital, but to no surprise, Clair and Hunter had been doing it most of their lives.

A few years had gone by after the first round of treatment, and they fell off the wagon — again, but this time both of them hit hard and with a loud thud. As before, Hunter's deal was drugs and alcohol; this go around Clair's was alcohol and him. He supplied the rest of the madness which drew her to him, and him to her, but it was also the madness that kept breaking them apart. In a bit of twisted irony, it was the madness that held them together.

The anguish Clair had experienced from birth until now —most of the anger and resentment was pushed deep inside. Drugs and alcohol helped her cope. She experimented with recreational drugs, no big deal, but alcohol became her closest friend as early as she could remember, and in her mind, pills didn't count. Hunter's was hardcore street drugs and everything that went with it. They both needed help, and for whatever reason, it was though the earth, moon, sun and stars were in perfect alignment for their combined decision.

They wanted and were willing to get rid of everything that had been holding them back once and for all. If Clair and Hunter could get to, or near a finish line, then they'd work out their relationship —if any was left.

Three months later after the failed dinner plans at Hunter's house, he and Clair walked through the front door of the Virginia Wolfe Wellness Center. It was a single-story, L-shaped building divided in two: druggies and alkies on one side— crazies on the other; She had a seat in both. This was her second time to go into treatment; Hunter had a season pass.

Treatment centers for many, was a temporary way to escape reality. They arrive at an emotionally sterile environment where everyone is taught to "feel and share," whichever side of the building you came from. Some get it, most don't. To those who don't, it was a waste of time and money. Clair and Hunter were representatives of both; she sought help, and he would have rather been doing something else, but willing to give it his best shot.

On the way to the center, they spoke their minds. There was a tenseness in the car, and to add to it, every cubic inch of breathable air was replaced with his cigarette smoke. A year ago, Clair quit smoking and let out a few fake coughs, fanned her face, and rolled down the window.

"Can you not smoke for one minute?"

"I guess I could, but don't wanna."

"Those things are going to kill you, and at this rate, you're taking me with you."

Clair did another phony cough, this time with more emphasis and stuck her head out the window to let the wind blow in her face. She pulled back inside, rolled up the window and turned the a/c on high.

"Can we please try to make this time more productive? Stop getting high all the time."

"Fine, then why don't you stop trying to kill yourself all the time! And while you're at it, slow down on the drinking."

Clair changed the rhetoric, shifted position in the car seat and turned toward him, scooted over, cradled his hand, and sweetly asked, "Hunter?"

He clasped hers and asked in a similar tone.

"Yes, Clair, what is it?"

She let go of his hand, moved back to her side, and replied not as sweetly.

"Go fuck yourself."

* * *

When they arrived, intake personnel greeted them.

"We have a ton of paperwork you need to fill out."

"Can't you use the one from the last time and change the date?"

Hunter thought he was amusing, the staff felt otherwise.

"Hunter, I see you haven't lost your wit. Here's a clipboard. Now do the paperwork."

As they were filling out the forms, Clair whispered, "Can't you ever be serious about anything? This is important."

Both had settled in, and Hunter knew the routine by heart. They had been at the treatment center for a week, and today was family visitation.

Hunter's words were soft and worried.

"Oh goodie."

Most of the family members gathered in the cafeteria and ate cake. Hunter was not easily rattled, but meeting with his folks was discomforting. They sat and waited and watched a clock as the second hand ticked away. Clair sensed his anxiety, patted him on his head like a little puppy dog, and assured him everything would be all right.

"I do not like that man," Hunter confided.

"You know, Clair, if he dropped dead right in front of me, I would be hard-pressed to shed a tear. Isn't that terrible?"

"I understand. I feel the same way about my brother."

She hadn't met his parents in the few years they'd been together, but today was the day. Seconds later, Hunter's parents arrived. His father was wearing surgical scrubs and his mother a tailored pantsuit. As soon as they spotted them, he and Clair rose to attention like soldiers greeting their general. They stopped halfway and met at the cake and punch table. Dr. Worcestershire shook Hunter's hand. His mom gave him an emotionless hug, then turned to Clair.

In a smug, measured tone, she stretched out her words.

"So, you... must... be... Clair."

"I... must... be," she replied in the same smug, measured tone.

Mrs. Worcestershire stayed in character.

"Nice to meet you, dear."

Clair responded in the same tone.

"Likewise, I'm sure."

Neither of them was certain about the other, but Clair was first to speak her mind, at least thought it.

"*What a bitch.*"

"Dear, will your family be visiting you today?"

"No, my family is dead."

"I'm so sorry. We'll be your family for the afternoon."

Clair smiled and nodded.

"Mom, dad, she's kidding. They're not all dead, just her father."

"That's not very respectful, is it, dear?"

"Depends on who's company you're keeping, isn't it Mrs. Worcestershire?"

Hunter almost passed out. He was already a nervous wreck, and the tension between Clair and his mother was bringing on a full-blown meltdown. To ease the stress, he invited them for some cake.

"Son, we have little time. I need to get back to the hospital..."

Interrupting him, Mrs. Worcestershire said she also had a benefit luncheon to attend. So much for quality time together and Clair's opportunity for a new family.

His father glanced at his watch, and without looking up, asked, "Do you think you can make this go-around stick?"

Hunter was silent, not knowing how to answer when his mom chimed in.

"Your father asked you a question, now answer him."

His father shifted his eyes from his watch, crossed his arms, and looked at him as if saying, "*I'm waiting.*"

Hunter felt like he was a victim of a Jeopardy question and responded, "*Let go and let God?*"

He hoped his clever, memorized quote would satisfy his parents and end the conversation. That hope quickly dashed.

They were standing alone, and his father commented that he was sick and tired of all the treatment jargon.

"Let go and let God, my ass! You, young man, need to pull your head out and get on with your life! I am growing weary of your bullshit, and all you can do is recite crap from a book!"

The quiet yelling continued, punctuated by a well-manicured finger aimed at Hunter.

"Acne is a disease. Asthma is a disease. Cancer, for Christ's sake, is a disease."

His tone quieted.

"What you have…" he said, pointing at the others, "… and those other losers is a lack of willpower!"

He looked at Clair and said, "You're not included. My understanding is that you're only a nut."

Clair showed complete contempt and responded with, "Gee whiz, Hank, thanks for clearing it up."

Henry was his first name and took advantage of it.

She had bitten her tongue throughout most of this exchange, but since the self-control genie was out of the bottle, Clair blurted out, "You really are an asshole."

"You, young missy, need to watch your tone. You have no idea what Dr. Worcestershire and I have been through."

She turned her attention to Hunter, and more calmly than her husband, said, "I agree with your father, you must grow up, and the time is now."

She paused for a moment, then asked, "How old are you?"

"In my twenties, Mother. Thanks for keeping up."

"My point exactly. We're not getting any younger."

Clair had heard enough.

"Yeah, Mrs. Worcestershire, I can tell it's taken a toll on you. It's written all over your face."

Hunter did everything he could to contain himself. Mrs. Worcester-shire gazed at Clair and didn't know if she was sympathetic, insulting or perhaps supportive. She was wrong, there was nothing supportive that came from Clair's mouth.

"Mom, dad, it will be all right, I promise."

"I guess we'll have to wait and see, now won't we?"

The feuding subsided, and Hunter led everyone to a sitting area. Along the way, he got a tray of coffee; three black and one with a single cube of sugar for his mother. By now, the two pairs had settled in for some small talk, and most of the tension left the room.

Some time back as a side investment, Hunter's father bought a small chain of full-service car washes and insisted Hunter takes an assistant manager position at one of them. He accepted and was paid an above-average salary for what he did. It was his father's way of weaning him off his bank account and hoped one day he developed enough interest to manage the whole thing. Wishful thinking on Dad's part. Hunter had little desire to work for his father, and zero interest in running a car wash, but smart enough to take the cash. He was worthless while at work and never missed when he wasn't.

Though art was her passion, Clair had a certificate degree in ac-counting and worked part time at a small bookkeeping service since the eleventh grade. When Clair met Hunter's parents, she did not know her employer did record keeping for Dr. Worcestershire's com-pany and his investments, but he knew of her. It was at that meeting, Dr. Worcestershire offered Clair a job after completing rehab, because in his words, he "liked her spunk."

Hunter's father knew of their relationship and asked if she would be interested in the accounting clerk position at the main office.

"Awww, that is so sweet of you to offer."

"You seem like a bright young woman, and I could use you on my team."

He slapped Hunter on the back, and at his expense, joked, "Maybe you can help me keep him in line."

Clair thought, "*Maybe I should take the job and steal your ass blind.*"

Instead of accepting his offer, declined and mumbled to herself, "*I wouldn't work for a piece of shit, ass wipe, no good, douche-bag imitation of a father like you. Wow! Who needs therapy? That felt great!*"

Chapter VIII

Hunter and Clair became treatment center superstars in the minds of many of the patients, and a few of the staff. They always took part in group sessions, led many twelve-step meetings and mentored several others, but this supposed good was a big joke. To some of the less naïve counselors, they were more like clowns in a circus.

They used their antics as a sideshow until they got there… wherever "there" was. Adding to their marching orders was their all-time favorite, "One fucking day at a time." Those were Hunter's and Clair's words, not out of a handbook, but even the appropriate saying didn't fly well with Dr. Worcestershire. Having made it to the ripe old age of twenty-eight, and outlasting the likes of Hendrix, Joplin, Mama Cass, and Morrison, each one dead at twenty-seven, they felt like newborns. While together in treatment and comparing themselves to the ever-growing dead celebrity list, their thinking was this could be a whole new beginning.

Hunter and Clair had a chat one day and discussed the abuse they went through as children. Both were victims of sexual abuse, but he one-upped her with the addition of almost daily beatings. He could still hear his mother's threat in his head when he did something wrong or misbehaved.

"You just wait until your father comes home, young man!"

Her words were as terrifying as the beatings — maybe more. But being excellent note-takers, they learned somewhere along the way their abusers were most likely abused, and those who did it to them were probably abused too. It remained a mystery if Hunter's or Clair's parents were ever abused; those things were never talked about. It wasn't proper to discuss family business, but it's a sure bet they were victims as well.

Hunter and Clair made a commitment to end the cycle of abuse and knew it had to start with them. They made a pledge to each other during a break from one of the therapy sessions.

They sat in the lobby, and Clair slid her chair in front of Hunter, held both of his hands, and looked him square in the eyes.

"This has got to stop, and we're the ones to do it. Are you with me?"

Determined, Hunter said, "You're right, Clair. It starts now."

She released his hands and sat up.

"Now don't you feel good about yourself?"

He shrugged his shoulders.

"I suppose."

They were pleased with their simple pledge, then both snickered when Hunter added, "This is the proudest moment of my life!"

"Me too!"

The two had accomplished little in their years, and a decision like this was a revelation. They sat back and relaxed before another session. Hunter was one of a handful who knew of Clair's attempts at hurting herself and endless desire to commit suicide. She always wore a light sweater or long-sleeved shirt to hide the scars, and while still sitting in the lobby, he turned to her and snatched one of her arms. He slid the sleeve up, exposing several healing cuts.

She tried to wiggle free from his grasp and asked in an elevated tone, "What the hell are you doing?" then under her breath exclaimed, "Let go of my arm!"

"Clair, you have to quit doing this shit to yourself and stop telling people the cat did it."

"And why not?"

She freed her arm and repositioned the sleeve back in place. All the while looking around to see if anyone saw her wounds, then moved her chair a few inches away from him.

Hunter said, "For one thing, you know I am allergic to cats."

"And?"

"You don't own a cat."

"OK, it was a neighbor's cat."

"Your building doesn't allow animals."

Throwing her arms in the air, and in a fit, concedes.

"All right, smart-ass! I'll tell them a fucking mountain lion did it! There! How's that?"

Hunter moved even further away from Clair, and said, "That'll do the trick. I'd go with it."

Although Hunter was a terrible boyfriend, he cared for her wellbeing and feared the worse. He knew there wasn't much he could do or say to prevent Clair from hurting or killing herself.

In a last effort, and perhaps his final plea, Hunter begged her. "Clair, promise me you will stop this."

Clair held her head down, and in her own sort of surrender, said, "I'm not sure I can make that promise and keep it."

* * *

Their days at the hospital were numbered. Clair was going to "graduate," and Hunter was getting kicked out... again. He felt the whole ordeal was a big waste of time, but knew she wanted this more than anything if it would help them and their relationship. Clair hadn't a clue where they were going or in what direction, but with more clarity than before, knew she didn't want to go back to wherever or whatever it used to be.

Clair stumbled and staggered toward the cliff's edge for many years, but what rattled her most was, as they say, hitting rock bottom. After years of wandering closer to the rocky abyss below, the dread of falling had waned; what she feared most was the sudden stop. She hadn't hit it yet, but damn sure knew where the drop-off was.

The day arrived for Clair and Hunter to say goodbye and were greeted by the staff and other patients. She was met by a senior counselor carrying roses and an AA handbook. He was marched out by an admin official with discharge papers and a bill.

The hospital held a brief 'letting go' ceremony. Clair passed her handbook around for them to sign like a high school yearbook. In it were the usual trite phrases. Stay clean and mean! One day at a time! You can do it! Keep praying to your higher power! One too many, a thousand never enough!

One inscription stood out from the rest. It read:

> Clair, it's up to you to chase away the demons. The decision is yours. Let them linger or let them go. Your friend, Suerenia.

She studied the words for a few moments. Tears followed. She wiped them away with the back of her hand and read the last few words again— *It's up to you.*

So far, not much was ever up to her, so she thought. Clair spent many years reflecting about most of her life, realizing what little control she had with it, at least it felt that way.

She pondered about her demons and Suerenia's words about chasing them away, then answered to herself, "*I hope so… if they let me.*"

After the ceremony, there were many tears, hugs, and some laughter. Clair gathered her things and tossed them into a green, military-style duffel bag and said goodbye to her temporary roommate. She got to the downstairs exit, threw the bag over her shoulder, made it to the parking lot, and saluted the security guard. Hunter was waiting for her at his car.

He leaned against it, and a cigarette hung from his mouth like a scene reminiscent of a James Dean movie.

"How was the party?"

"Same as the last time. Let's get out of here," she said while tossing the bag in the backseat.

Chapter IX

It had been almost six months since they left the hospital. Clair stopped drinking and even went back to a few AA meetings with a different attitude than before and took a break from trying to hurt herself. Hunter also went to an occasional support group for drug addicts, but his reason was to pick up girls. She has not seen him since leaving rehab because they chilled down the relationship until they felt the time was right, so, for now, she had the chance to dabble with some of her paintings without interference.

Clair was working on one of her projects and took a break for some hot tea. She sat alone studying her art and worried about the direction it was going, or in this case... not going. So far it wasn't much, just a few pencil sketches with no shape, rhyme or reason.

"I suppose I'll go with my gut on this one."

She held the cup to her mouth, blew the hot liquid to cool it and took the first cautious sip.

Cup still in hand, she took another sip but forgot to blow.

"Dammit!"

Then spit the remains of the hot liquid back in the cup and lowered it toward the end table. On the way down, some of it spilled on her bare legs.

"Holy shit!"

She cleaned herself, stood up, walked toward the canvass, then stared at it and said aloud, "What are you saying? Talk to me! What do you want me to do?"

Clair gazed at it for an answer.

"So, it's come down to this, —" and laughed —, "I really am crazy! I'm having a conversation with pulp!"

There was a tap on the door. It was more of a knock-knock.

Clair lifted herself from the chair and asked, "Who's there?"

She opened the door with the security chain still doing its job and cracked it open enough to see who was there.

"Miss Reynolds, special delivery. I need a signature."

She unlatched the chain, and instead of placing it on its little holder, she let it fall.

It swung back and forth like a pendulum, then flung the door wide open, and asked, "Who's it from?"

In a rude tone, he replied, "I don't know, lady, they pay me to deliver, not to read the details."

He handed her a small box wrapped in butcher block paper and sealed with an endless roll of tape. The driver handed over a clipboard for her to sign the proof of delivery ticket. She signed the paper and handed it back. He tucked the clipboard and document under his left arm, then extended his right hand, palm side up, hinting at a tip.

While slamming the door in his face, she said, "You have got to be kidding me."

Clair looked at the small package with curiosity.

"What have we here?"

Using the same X-acto knife as before, she cut through the tape and revealed its contents; one was a letter, the other was a small painting. She read the note aloud.

Ms. Reynolds,

We regret to inform you that your submission to the art contest did not meet our criteria for consideration. After a careful review of your work, our judging panel concluded it was weak on several levels. Your lines were not clear, and the coloring is annoying. Better luck next time.

Yours sincerely,

Madison Goodread, Curator, Bayview County Art Museum

At first, she was a little stunned and said nothing. Then it came.

"You snotty little bastard!"

She read the note one more time, laughed, crumpled it, and tossed the wadded note and the piece of art in the trash. She would have cried, but instead recalled something she'd read awhile back. It was a story about a gorilla that did a painting. They gave him an artist's palette with a dozen colors. His handlers gave the gorilla a brush and an hour to finish. When it was completed, or when they thought it was completed, tossed him a banana. But the study wasn't over with. His trainer took the piece to the same museum that rejected her and presented the work from an unknown painter. The curator was informed about the experiment and who the artist was.

The museum used the event as a fundraiser and held a formal cocktail party to celebrate this "masterpiece." Patrons, board members, and invited guests eagerly lined up for the unveiling. The painting was concealed with a black, satin drape. One of the museum workers removed it and flung the covering like a magician revealing the rabbit and stepped away from the painting, giving the piece its proper due.

Those in attendance let out a big *oooh* and *awww*.

"It speaks to me!" said one guest.

"A spectacle of color!" another shouted.

And lastly, "Dazzling imagery!"

When the curator announced the experiment, the chatter from the crowd silenced. Several slammed their champagne in single gulps; the rest took another from the waiter's cocktail tray in ones and twos.

A lady in a full-length mink coat shouted, "Well, I never!" Then turned and walked out, followed by her wimpy, little husband.

The others continued viewing the painting, and the board president of the Bayview County Art Museum seized the arm of the curator, saying he'd like to have a word with him. He led him away like a teacher hauling a kid off to the principal's office… certainly not to discuss a pay raise.

That would explain her laughter, but numbed with more continued defeat.

Clair had been seeing a therapist for some time. His name was Glenn. He was tall; about six feet, thin, jet black hair and eyes to match. In Clair's opinion and a few others, Glenn was kind of a nerd, but to Clair, he was nerdy, cool, and asked herself if it was even possible. His clothes looked like they came from a yard sale and he used outdated words and expressions, but somehow, they always communicated.

She hadn't talked to Glenn for some time and wanted to have a chat and called his office on his direct line.

"Hello, this is Glenn. I'm not available to take your call. Leave me a message and I will call you back when it's convenient. Have a clean and sober day."

"When it's convenient? What an asshole!"

She slammed the phone, looked at the blank canvas, and had another conversation with it.

"Let me get this straight…." then paced around.

"I work my ass off, put thought and emotion into my art, work for days, weeks, sometimes months, and a damn ape with a paintbrush got more accolades than me?"

Clair continued the rant with, "Maybe I should wear a damn monkey suit and sit on a street corner."

She calmed down and sat back on the chair. By now the tea had cooled, took a swig, then the phone rang. Glancing at the caller ID info, it displayed, 'unknown.' Thinking it may be a telemarketing call, answered with her memorized response.

"Clair isn't home, she died in the war."

The caller laughed and said, "Hey, Clair, it's Glenn. Don't hang up."

She perked up after hearing his voice.

"Oh, Hi Glenn. How are you?"

"I'm swell. You called? Is everything hunky-dory?"

He sounded concerned, but if he wasn't, he was hiding it well.

Mocking his words, she said, "Just peachy! I got another rejection letter."

Then plopped in her chair.

"From the museum?"

"No, Glenn, from the five and dime. Of course the museum."

He gave her his fullest attention and leaned forward from his chair.

"Aren't we being a little defensive?"

Clair had heard that tone from him before and imagined his face, suspecting he was doing his best not to grin maintaining a serious expression —and failing at it.

Changing position in her chair, sat up with both feet planted on the floor.

"No, we're not being defensive… I am."

Clair settled down, slumped back, tucked both legs under, and sat cross-legged.

"I'm sorry. It pisses me off that the more I try, the more disappointed I get."

Using words of wisdom, Glenn said, "No. Try not. Do. Or do not. There is no try."

"That sounds familiar. Where have I heard it?" Clair asked.

"Star Wars. It was a quote from Yoda."

"Oh yeah, I remember. I loved Star Wars."

Then, Glenn changed the tone of the conversation.

"You don't want to hurt yourself, do you?"

She uncrossed her legs and sat up again.

"No, but I want to punch someone in the throat!"

"Expressing your anger is helpful."

With a hint of a snicker and with the voice of an innocent child, asked, "You want to stop by?"

"I think I'll pass," he said with a chuckle.

Clair walked to a nearby window and peeked out.

"I have to go and work on another loser piece of shit. I'll talk to you later."

"Anytime, Clair. Bye now."

She removed the phone from her ear and stared at it, put it back to her ear and said, "Wait a second. Anytime, Clair? Bye now?'"

Glenn seemed confused and asked, "What do you mean?"

With the phone held in place, using her shoulder and cheek to keep it there, walked toward her unfinished canvas and picked it up.

"I was expecting more from Yoda."

"I don't understand. You're the one who said you needed to go, I was accommodating the request."

"Yeah, but…"

"But what?"

He cleared his throat and recited another Yoda impression.

"Possess in you, tools you have, young Jedi."

"That was the worst Yoda I've ever heard."

She laughed after placing the unfinished work back on its easel.

"You are a far better therapist than an actor, but you're right; I called you. That's a good thing, isn't it?"

"Yes, it is. I'm just one of the tools in your toolbox. Now, I should go. Got a meeting in five."

"Thanks a lot, Glenn, I mean it." And she did.

"No sweat. You're welcome, Clair."

There was a pause and no goodbyes; they simply hung up.

Chapter X

Clair had more bouts with anxiety and called Glenn many times when she was down. The last phone chat with her, he suggested she attends one of his outpatient programs. During the conversation, Clair told him she wanted to toss out the prescribed pills and face her life head on without interference. Glenn suggested talking to her doctor first.

The group members gathered twice a week in a small, dimly lit room at the treatment center. It had stark, clinical white walls, and the ceiling painted a hideous shade of green, like watery pea soup, and the whole place smelled of disinfectant. On the walls hung the typical trappings: a framed copy of The Serenity Prayer, the AA symbol, and a large, full color poster of a unicorn. The chairs were lined up in a semi-circle; the furthest one was against a wall in a windowless room, and that is where Clair sat —smack dab in the middle. Glenn was positioned in the center, facing the rest of the attendees and straight across from Clair about ten feet away.

After weeks and a dozen meetings, she zeroed in about what her life meant to her, focusing on the past. She was always mindful of what Suerenia wrote in her book about letting go of her demons and those thoughts that haunted her, but this time in a pleasant way.

"It's all under control."

There were ten in the group including Glenn. He began the session with a brief, "So how are you folks doing today?"

And like little smart-ass elementary students, they replied in unison, "Very well, teacher."

Counselors are trained 'ignorers,' except for those things that matter, and not much seems to get under their skin. They are more like trained seals, but Clair liked Glenn. He was a quiet man and an excellent therapist, but when you get him going —he's like a dog on a bone.

"Before we get started today, we have a little business to discuss. Clair, I understand you and Hunter raided a sex addict meeting."

"So."

"How appropriate is it to ask the group," —then looking at his notes — "who wants to relapse?"

"It was fun," she said with a hint of nervousness.

"Could you two please entertain yourselves with something else, like maybe go to a zoo?"

"You mean like this place?"

"Very amusing, Clair. And while you're at it, please stop referring to the codependent patients as —" he does a quick scan of his notes again — "let me see here…, oh yes, 'those poor sick, half-crazed bastards.' "

Embarrassed, she again let out a nervous giggle.

"Well, they are. They can't breathe in and out without approval."

Suerenia was always quiet and reserved but had something to say.

"Clair, how can you be so judgmental? I'm sorry, but you're not here because you are the poster child for mental stability."

Clair said nothing because she knew Suerenia was right.

Glenn sat and listened to Suerenia with approval, then said to Clair, "Do me a favor, keep your insults to yourself and leave the other groups alone. They have their struggles just like you. One more thing, Larry, I heard about your cousin. You have my sincerest condolence."

Lisa asked, "What happened?"

"My cousin, Earnest passed away."

Lauren responded, "That's terrible!"

Glenn got up from his chair, walked over to Larry and placed a comforting hand on his shoulder. He responded with compassion and soft-spoken words.

"Larry, I am sorry your cousin died, but that's not passing away —he got shot. Knowing the difference will help you in the grieving process."

He knew of the circumstances involved in his death and aware he was killed during a rival gang confrontation. Glenn returned to his seat to finish the conversation.

"It tickles me — not in a rude way, but some confuse the term. The same thing with a suicide. I'd hear the same rhetoric that, so-and-so passed away when I knew damn well they killed themselves."

Clair jumped to her feet.

"How can you be so cruel?"

"Cruel? I'm just stating the facts. Again, suicide is not passing away —one got gunned down, and the other one blew their damn brains out! Mostly they are decisions. One was at the wrong place at the wrong time, the other decided to 'check out' on their own."

Clair sat down and muttered, "Semantics."

"No, Clair, it isn't. Passing away is something you do in your sleep or drop dead because of a heart attack or extended illness… that's passing away. It's nature's way of saying it's time to slow down."

Blake commented, "Yeah, way down,"

Glenn glanced at the clock.

"Any questions or comments?"

"I have one."

"Yes, what is it, Clair?"

"Glenn, you're an idiot."

"Thank you, Clair. I will take it under advisement. Alrighty then, enough of that. Let's get started. Who wants to go first?"

There was silence.

"Clair, we'll start with you."

"Why me? What did I do? You're just mad at me; besides, today is my birthday —the big two-eight."

"I'll address each. First off, I run the group, not you. Second, I didn't suggest you did anything. Third, I don't get mad, and by the way, happy birthday. Do you want us to sing you a song?"

"I'm good, I have the album. I'll play it later. Start with Larry, he's the most fucked up one in the room."

"That's not very nice, now is it?"

"Clair's right. I am the most fucked up."

Everyone in the room burst out laughing, including Larry, and not his usual style... Glenn did too, then got the group to refocus.

"All right folks, let's get serious. So, Larry, why don't you lead us off and tell us how your day has been going so far."

He told the others' how good he'd been dealing with his anger and reported he hadn't hit anyone today.

Not his usual style but Glenn said with a hint of sarcasm, "We're very grateful, Larry. Keep up the good work."

The group members let out an enthusiastic applause. Larry stood up and took a bow.

At receiving such accolades, he smiled and said, "I also haven't thought about cutting off my mother's head or stabbing the rest of my family to death either."

That didn't get an applause, only silence and stares, but it didn't stop Glenn and remained professional with his continued comment.

"Larry, that is also something to be proud of."

Glenn pretended to take a note and whispered to himself, "Psycho."

Glenn got back to being the skilled therapist and added, "Larry, so you know, the gash on the janitor's face is healing quite nicely. He's able to eat solid food again."

"I said I was sorry. Did he get my card?"

"Yes, he did. It was very thoughtful. Clair, you're next. How was your day?"

Slumped and relaxed in her seat, responded, "Fine."

Glenn leaned back in his chair and crossed his arms.

"Fine? Okay, group, we all know what that means, don't we?"

After the question, they chanted, "Fucked up, Insecure, Neurotic, and Emotional!"

Not amused, she responded, "Ha, ha, ha. That's hysterical. I'm all right. Thanks for asking. Can we please move this thing along?"

"What a great idea."

Glenn gazed around at the others, then looked at Clair.

"I want to ask you a question."

Still slumped in her chair, said, "Shoot."

Larry jumped out of his chair and exclaimed, "Shoot who?"

Mike, another one of the group members, said, "It's an expression. It means I'm giving you permission to proceed. So, sit your fat ass down and shut up!"

Larry complied, but also made a gesture with his pointer and middle finger, aimed at his eyes, and motioned in return with the implication, "I'm watching you."

Mike looked at him and shook his head.

"Larry, go to hell."

"Okay, fellows, let's keep the testosterone to a manageable level. Let's get started again, and can we try it with no more interruptions? Clair?"

She stood up at attention and saluted.

"Yes, Comrade Counselor?"

The room erupted with slight laughter.

"Please sit down."

"Ya Vol, Mein Fuhrer!"

Obeying his command, she sat down and again slumped in her chair, but now both feet were kicked straight out, rigid and crossed.

Glenn wasted no time, remained poised, and got straight to it.

"Clair, I want to ask you a question; who are your demons?"

Pondering the question, she replied, "I don't know, maybe the boogeyman."

More chuckles from the participants, but it gave her a moment of pause, remembering back when Edward said it to her.

He repeated the question, implying he would not settle for another smart-ass answer.

"Clair, who are your demons?"

There was a hushed silent in the room, and every eye was on her. She acted as though she didn't hear the question this time. To add to her posture, her arms were now tightly squeezed across her chest.

Still calm, and without changes in his tone, Glenn asked again, "Who are your demons?"

She remained in her defensive stance —but now her arms grew tighter, legs remained outstretched... also crossed, and added a hint of nervous foot twitching.

"Clair, I asked you a question."

She swelled up inside and was about to burst wide open, but managed a calm, chilled retort.

"Back off, Glenn."

"Who are your demons?" he asked again.

Now less calm, she said, "I swear to God, you are really starting to irritate me."

"Clair, I can't make you feel anything. It belongs to you."

"You're right, you can't. But, you can stick that therapy shit up your ass, because right now, you're pissing me off!"

Glenn remained poised.

"Clair, please stay focused and answer the question."

She sat up and uncrossed her feet and planted them on the floor. And with outstretched arms, she flung them with each word.

"What, Glenn? What do you want me to say?"

Clair is running out of room to hide and is feeling attacked. He knows it and perseveres.

"I don't want you to say something; I want you to tell me and the others. I'll ask it one more time. Clair, who are your dem..."

Before he could finish the question, she jumped up from her chair and yelled at the top of her lungs, "Everyone! Everyone is a fucking demon! Are you happy now?"

Angry and frustrated, she dropped onto the chair with so much force it hit the wall with a loud bang. The room went silent.

"I can see you're upset."

She lowered her head and said, "No shit."

"But who are you the angriest with? Surely not all of us —" and in a rare stab at a little humor, he finished with — "except maybe me." That brought a brief smile on her face.

She got back to her relaxed posture.

"I guess I'm the angriest at Hunter."

"Isn't that a little too easy? You really think Hunter is one of your demons."

"He's damn sure no saint."

"When you guys are together and getting along, aren't you happy?"

"I guess."

"Let's rule him out. What about your father?"

"You mean the sperm donor? He's dead."

"Yes, I know. Before then. Is your father one of your demons?"

"Not really, I just hate him."

"And your mother?"

"No, I only despise her."

"What about Edward, your brother?"

Clair paused for a moment, sat up, then looked Glenn straight in the eyes, and in a voice of calm, said, "I would like to see him tortured to death and cut into little pieces."

"Now we're getting somewhere."

Larry jumped up and raised his hand.

"Can I help?"

If any help were needed, Glenn told him she'd call.

"I'll let you in on a little secret, Clair. Edward is not one of your demons either."

"Then, who is? You seem to know everything else. Who are my demons?"

"All of those you mentioned are only distractions and not letting you see who they truly are."

"What do you mean?"

"I'll show you."

Glenn reached under his chair and slid an object on the floor toward Clair. It got to its mark, and she picked it up.

"I've had a ton of practice." Referring to her and Charlies' shuffle-board routine with the drinks.

"OK, now what?"

"Hold it up."

She held the object at eye level with her arms bent to get a good view.

"Now, turn it around."

As she did, her reflection appeared and peeked for a moment then sat it on her lap.

"Clair, pick it up. Look at it again and listen to what I am saying."

She picked it up and held it as before. "What do you see?"

"Me."

"Yes, you are right, it is you, but tell us what you see. Describe it to us."

"I can't."

She slammed the mirror back on her lap again.

"Why are you such a jerk?"

"I'm paid to be your therapist, not your friend. I have to practice the jerk part."

"You're doing a good job."

He ignored the jab and told her to pick up the mirror again and look at it.

As she did, he asked the others, "Now group, let's help her out. Lisa, what do you see?"

"She's pretty."

"Mark?"

"She's smart."

"Suerenia?"

"She's always been a kind friend."

Clair lowered the mirror and Glenn said, "Keep looking."

She raised the mirror back in position and listened to other group members. A slight sniffle was heard, followed by a small trail of goo coming from her nose, and hoping no one noticed, wiped it clean.

Glenn asked, "Do you need a tissue?"

"No thanks. My sleeve will do."

"Okeydokey, let's get back to it. Blake, what do you think?"

"Her eyes are gorgeous."

Now a tear rolled down her cheek, followed by another. Clair was unable or unwilling to see what they saw but tried to absorb each word they said. Saying something good about what was in the mirror was contrary to what she believed.

"And you two? What do you boys think?"

Ryan and Jason said together as if they rehearsed it, "She's hot!"

That made her chuckle in between sniffles.

"Lauren, your thoughts?"

"I would kill for that hair!"

Larry again jumped to his feet again, "Right on, sister!"

"Sit down Larry and relax."

Glenn didn't want to leave him out of the exercise, but with reluctance asked him the same question. He seemed put off and not very enthusiastic.

He yawned and said, "OK, Larry, tell us something about Clair."

Not in his usual, obnoxious behavior, he said with great sincerity, "I wish Clair was my girl."

It's hard to explain, but Larry's answer got her tears to flow.

Clair got up from the chair, went over to Larry, put her arms around him, and gave a big hug, then whispered, "Thank you, Larry," then kissed him on the cheek and returned to her seat.

She settled in, only this time, and on her own, got the mirror back in position.

"Clair, I'll ask you one last time, who are your demons? Take your time."

The group waited as she gazed into the mirror. She stared for a few more moments and let out a sigh. The others sat in deafening silence waiting for her answer.

Glenn already knew, but instead said, "Clair, please, tell the group who they are," and said to himself, "Come on Clair, you can do it."

The wheels started to turn, and the power the demons had on her were becoming weaker and weaker. Clair stared at the reflection, and as she did, millions of images raced through her brain like a high-speed movie projector. All the way from childhood until now seemed to pass right in front of her mind's eye within those few moments.

"Clair?"

All the while, she hadn't moved and continued to stare, then quietly announced, "I know who the demon is. There is only one."

Glenn leaned forward.

"And who might that be?"

Everyone had remained quiet this whole time, then Suerenia whispered, "Clair, tell him."

Clair took a quick glance at Suerenia, paused, then lowered the mirror and placed it on her lap.

She let out another deep sigh, then in a soft tone said, "Me, I'm the demon."

The room again went silent except for a collective exhale. You could hear a pin drop because the group knew this was a crossroad for Clair. She finally met her demon face to face and prepared to challenge it.

"Clair, what you see in the mirror is the face of torment. You are not the demon. The past that haunts you is, and I want you to know the difference. What you saw was an image of its representative, and that's all. It's not real —only a reflection. But when you put into your head harmful thinking, you give it a reason to live. Your actions, like trying to kill yourself, are nourishment for the demon, and you must starve it. Now, you call the shots —" then Glenn emphasized — "because you are now in control, not an image in a mirror. Pick it up again."

Clair raised the mirror, looked into it, but this time with a hint of a smile.

"Now what do you see?"

She paused for a moment, then let out a comforting sigh and said, "I see hope."

"Me too. Good work. I'm very proud of you."

Her response was short and somber.

"Thank you, Glenn," and she meant it.

Chapter XI

The rest of the group departed and went for coffee; Larry had to report to his parole officer. Glenn and Clair were left alone.

"You did an excellent job today."

Somewhat sniffly, nodded and said, "Yeah, it was a blast. When can we do that again?"

Glenn could tell that she was still upset. He reached into another drawer and pulled out a bottled water.

"You want one?"

"Sure."

He got another one and twisted the cap enough to break the seal and handed it to her.

"Thanks. I need a stiff H2O."

Clair lifted the bottle and gave a toast.

"Cheers," then took a long drink of the water.

A few minutes went by, and he gave Clair enough time to relax and settle down.

"Have you ever heard the saying, 'I complained I had no shoes until I met a man with no feet?' "

"That's a hell of a way to begin a conversation. Yes, I have. Haven't we all?"

"But did you ever think about it and what the meaning might be?"

"I guess to be grateful for what you have."

"That's what they want you to think."

"Huh?"

"If you ponder on it for a moment, it goes much deeper."

Rolling her eyes, she said, "Sure it does."

Glenn continued.

"On the surface, we look around and see that some lives are better... some worse; then we compare the two. It boils down to this. I'm sorry you don't have feet, and it's not my fault, but mine are cold, and I need a pair of shoes."

"That sounds harsh."

"No, it isn't, and I'll tell you why. You must take care of yourself first before you can take care of anyone else."

"It sounds selfish."

"You're right. In my line of work, we have to teach selfishness. Many people suffer many things, and it's easy to empathize. But your pain is personal, you own it. No one can fix it except you. Put yourself above everyone else and protect what is inside you."

"I think I understand."

"Good. Because it can save your life."

Then out of the blue, he asked, "Clair, why do you want to kill yourself?"

"Wow! Where did that come from?"

Clair was no stranger to suicide. She had so many friends and family members who killed themselves, amused herself and said that it must be contagious.

She thought about his question for several minutes, and he waited for her answer never saying a word, then said, "It is so difficult to say why. Sometimes it just seems right, like the short way out. I had a friend who was one of the happiest women I ever knew; always smiling and joking around. Everyone loved and respected her, I suppose everyone except herself. One day I got a call from her husband asking if I knew where she was; I didn't."

Clair teared up, and Glenn noticed.

"You all right?"

She ignored the question.

"The next day her husband called and said they found her body."

Clair was weeping and said, "She killed herself! I couldn't think and said nothing. It was though time froze and all I could do was fall to the floor and cry. She had two little kids for God's sake! How could anyone do that?"

"Clair, she did it to herself, not them. Are you getting it? I'll lay odds she never knew anyone cared for her, but you did, and I'm sure many others did too."

"Yes, she had many friends."

"My guess is no one knew why she killed herself, did they?"

"Some have speculated."

Glenn seemed to get angry and irritated.

"Speculation is not enough. We must sort this out and learn better how to treat it. There is always an epicenter leading to suicide, and depression and other things lead to it, and I prefer that you not be one of them."

He warned Clair that she would never be forever rid of what haunts her. Destructive behavior and suicidal thoughts would always be trouble signs to watch for. Self-doubt, anxiety and depression go on vacation, sometimes for a day, a few weeks and perhaps years, but rarely take a permanent time out. You learn to cope with it and keep things in perspective. He also cautioned her that many times family members, and a few others, helped get her where she was in life.

"The past and whoever harmed you is not your definition. Recognizing and reconciling with it can give you the strength to be who you really are, and for way too many, they are lost and get overshadowed because of it."

"That sounds very nice, but what in the hell are you saying?"

"Throw all the shit out of your life that got you here. Be the first in line to come and realize you have worth and meaning."

"Why didn't you say that in the first place?"

"Because I'm a therapist. That's not how we're supposed to say it. So, Clair, what do you think?"

"I'm paying you. What do you think?"

"I can't tell you what I think, only what I know. All of those people who ever hurt you— that was their fault —" then pointing at her — "and not yours."

Clair lowered her head and said, "I know."

"Do you? You think for one second that a little kid can defend herself from an overpowering brother or parents who humiliated her?"

"I suppose not."

"Suppose not! For crying out loud, Clair, you were a child for Christ's sake! You have been carting around so much guilt and shame your whole life. I'm amazed you've made it this far. You are a good person and deserve to be happy. You need to invite people into your life that are uplifting and honest, not the ones who hurt and belittle. I had a client a few years back; I still remember her name. It was Courtney. I swear to God, you two could have been sisters in a parallel universe. You even look alike."

She took in every word he spoke, more than almost anything else he ever said.

"But how do I handle those who are already around me?"

"That's easy. You have new rules to live by and rule number one is they must obey your rules or have nothing to do with them — and I don't care who. Most of the clients I have met are usually the wrong ones in therapy."

Curious, she asked, "What do you mean?"

"Don't get me wrong, they need help to get a handle on things and try to make sense out of everything, but sometimes it's the people in and around their lives that got them here in the first place. Most of the time, it's their nut-job family. Hell, I've met your mother, and she's a few cards short of a full deck."

Clair laughed, but Glenn felt an angry rant coming on — instead, he laughed too.

"All I'm saying, is you and many others in this place are here because of some bullshit along the way. Over time, their emotions have been trampled so hard and heavy they have little left to stomp."

Throughout this conversation, the roles seemed to have swapped.

"Sometimes I have to turn off my emotions when I hear some of the stuff they tell me, and so much of it hurts my heart. I am amazed what people can do to each other."

"How does it make you feel?"

"Like shit! Wait a minute…"

In a rare comedic moment, he said, "I'm the therapist, you can't ask me that."

Clair busted out laughing.

"Yeah, I know. I can't believe they pay you people for asking a few dumb questions."

"You know what? You're probably right."

Her laughter stopped and held back a grin.

"Why do you think that is?"

"Oh, you know…."

He looked at her, and Clair couldn't hold a straight face any longer, and in his best Jack Benny impersonation, Glenn said, "Now, cut that out!"

That set off more laughter between them. They chatted a little more, looked at each other, and she left.

On her way out, she thought, "*I really like him.*"

Though he was paid, Glenn was only one of a handful that stayed by Clair's side; others cut and ran. It takes a special someone to go for the ride with folks suffering from mental illness.

* * *

Glenn had a lecture later in the afternoon and explained to everyone in attendance what mental illness was and what it wasn't. Clair sat on the front row.

In his lecture, he said, "You wouldn't take off and pluck someone out of your life you care for who has cancer. Why should it be any different with someone who suffers mental disease? It takes strength and perseverance to give comfort and support to someone who wants to sabotage their efforts to heal and move on."

He continued.

"But sometimes you watch from the outside and see a friend or a loved one staying stuck where they are and never seem to try or even care about moving forward. Then worry, fear and concern kick in when they reverse the course and go in the other direction. Those are the ones to watch."

Hunter was as screwed up as Clair; sometimes worse, but most times only by a fraction of an inch either way, but it was still hard for him to watch her fall. He was not a role model for recovery, but he was one of the few that stuck around.

Chapter XII

Glenn helped Clair to get on the right track, but trains never go on a straight path, and he knew it. There are hills to climb and curves to maneuver, and sometimes the train derails, and when it does, he hoped Clair had enough knowledge and information to find the track and get back on. In his line of work, he knew the majority would fall off and seldom return. Clair was not an exception; for her, more demons lay ahead.

* * *

Clair continued to stay away from pills, alcohol, and suicidal ideas and put a permanent end to her relationship with Hunter. They still chatted on the phone occasionally, but had enough sense to keep her distance, and tried to put her life back together; she wanted no interference from him. It was hard on her at first, but learned to manage.

She had an occasional fling with some of her art pals, and in her words, "To get my tires rotated now and then."

One of her romances almost got serious, but cut it off before it went anywhere.

After a few months of solitude, Clair settled back into some of the things that got her into trouble. She started her earlier routine of going to McDonald's and the bar, but decided no whiskey and only one bottle of beer. Clair stuck with her decision of the one beer policy for several weeks, proving to herself she could handle it. Each time she went during those few weeks, Clair spent two, sometimes three hours sipping each drop of beer like nectar from the gods. Toward the end of each evening, the beer went from an ice-cold beverage to a lukewarm slurry. At the bottom of the bottle, was a stale, undesirable lather, then slammed the last gulp.

"*Arrrggg!* That was terrible!" she said every time and after every last gulp.

She kept her word and remained committed to the "just one" policy.

One evening, Charlie asked, "Clair, you have been coming in here a lot, and I know some of what you went through."

As usual, Charlie wiped the bar.

Then he asked, "Do you think this is a wise idea?"

"I'll be all right. I know what I'm doing."

She laughed and continued.

"How much trouble can one little ole' beer get me into?"

Clair kept this going for several weeks and then it happened. As they say in the drug and alcohol self-help groups, "one too many, a thousand never enough." Clair tested it to its limit and had a monolithic setback. Though she felt the demon had been dealt with, it returned, but this time, it brought along a few pals. On this evening, she fell off the wagon... again, but instead of falling, she jumped, the wagon ran over her, backed up, and rolled over her again, but for this event, it was whiskey and pills and plenty of both. Whether Clair believed it or not, she almost accomplished her suicidal wish.

For whatever reason, something had been bugging Hunter, almost like a premonition. He hadn't talked to Clair for a few days and called. He punched in her number, and it rang a dozen times with no answer. Hunter knew she was home, so after several phone attempts, he went to her apartment. He arrived at her front door and rang the doorbell. Nothing. This time, he pounded the hell out of it with so much force he heard the door frame crack.

"Clair, open the door! I mean it! Open the damn door!"

Still nothing. He went around to the back of the apartment to her studio, broke out a window, unlatched it, and crawled in. He ran to the front part and found her in the bedroom; laying spread out on the floor, unconscious and her breathing was shallow and sporadic.

"Oh my God, Clair!" Then exclaimed, "What have you done this time?"

Pills were all over the place, and tight in her hand was a bottle of booze. Hunter dialed 911 and reported a possible overdose. The operator asked if he knew what kind of pills they were.

"Xanax. She was being treated for anxiety and depression."

"Do you know how many she took?"

He was in a panic and tried to assess the number of pills as quick as he could. It was a recent prescription with a thirty count on the label. He guesstimated there was about ten, maybe fifteen on the floor; meaning Clair had taken almost half of them or more.

"Anything else? I mean, did she take them with anything?"

"Yes —booze, and it looks like a lot!"

"The EMTs are on the way."

Hunter hung up the phone, picked her up, and placed her on the bed. He cradled her in his lap and stroked her hair. Tears were rolling down his face with the realization she may not be part of his life anymore.

Sobbing, he said, "Please don't do this to me. I'm begging you. Stay with me, Clair! Please!"

Through his sobs, he heard a siren getting louder and louder, then stop. A few seconds later, the EMTs were knocking at the door. He ran down the hallway, swung it open, and they rushed to her bedside. They checked her vital signs.

"It's a good thing you called when you did because there is not much time. You may have saved this woman's life."

They loaded her on a gurney and started an IV drip.

"The police will meet you at the hospital."

"The police? Why?"

"Anytime we suspect someone tried to commit suicide, they have to be notified. A homicide detective will need to get a statement from you."

"Why a homicide detective?"

"Yeah, I know. Funny, isn't it? They do double duty."

"And what makes you think this was a suicide attempt?"

"Look around, sir, then ask me again."

Hunter took a quick glance around the room.

"I see your point."

"We have to hurry. The medical staff will probably do a gastric lavage at the ER, I'm almost certain."

"What's that?"

"Pump her stomach… if she makes it."

They wheeled her out of the apartment and loaded her into the back of the ambulance. They let Hunter go along for the trip. One of the EMTs noticed a make-shift bandage that hid a large cut on Hunter's arm from the broken glass he busted.

"You are going to need a few stitches. Let me look at it."

"Just tend to her. I'll deal with this later."

The ambulance arrived at the hospital and screeched to a halt, leaving skid marks in its wake. The back door of the ambulance swung open, she was unloaded, and the ER team took over, but if it hadn't been for Hunter, this would have ended right here. She's dead —The End.

After a few hours of working on her, they got Clair stabilized, and Hunter came to see her. The hospital staff moved her to a regular patient room, and she laid flat on her back gazing out the window.

"Clair?"

She ignored him and continued to stare.

"Are you okay?"

She turned and glared at him.

"No, I'm not okay," then turned back toward the window and muttered, "Why don't you leave me alone."

"You, ungrateful little bitch! Maybe I should have left you alone."

Pointing toward her apartment, he said, "I wish I'd never gone there. I should have let someone else deal with your crap!"

"Maybe you should have."

She let out a big sigh and said, "I would have been better off dead."

"Is that what you want? Do you think you will win a toaster for having the shittiest life ever? You think you're it?"

Clair continued to ignore him.

"You don't know how many times I wanted to blow my fucking brains out. You think you have an exclusive with misery in your life… I've had plenty. But I want to figure it out and live. You kill yourself, then that's, that, but for us who care would like for you to stick around."

She turned away from the window and looked at Hunter.

"I do want to live; I don't know how."

"Sometimes we just need to breathe and relax and enjoy what's around us."

"How's that working out for you?"

"Like I said, Clair, I'm trying."

He walked over to her bedside and held her hand.

"You were doing so good. I called your mom. She should be here any minute."

She released his hand and pushed it away.

"Fantastic, I can't wait to see her."

"She's worried about you."

"I'm *soooo* sure."

"I also called your therapist."

Still weak, she struggled to sit up.

"Why in the hell would you call Glenn?"

"Because he needed to know, that's why."

"This is bullshit!"

Then fell back on the bed.

He left her room without saying goodbye. A few steps down the hallway, he crossed paths with her mother and asked how she was.

Still walking and not stopping, he said, "She's alive," and continued to walk toward the exit.

The visit with Clair was brief. Her mother was concerned and appeared to care, but caring and concern, at least in Clair's opinion, it was a moot point and out of character; just a charitable event and nothing else.

Chapter XIII

The next day, Clair was in the discharge area of the hospital waiting for her ride. She sat on a padded vinyl bench in a slumped position, rubbing her throat up and down trying to massage away the soreness from the tubes they shoved down her throat when they pumped her stomach.

The large windows allowed in so much sunlight, she reached into her handbag for sunglasses. With decorative plants everywhere, and people walking all around, it seemed surreal; almost like a dream.

Clair continued to wait and was expecting Hunter; instead, it was Glenn. He sat beside her, and she moved as far away as possible without falling off the edge. Neither had a word to say. This went on for several minutes.

Glenn was the first to break the silence.

"I never told you this, but my mother killed herself when I was twelve."

Clair turned toward him in a bit of shock.

"I'm sorry. I wasn't aware."

"Now you are. No one knew why, not even my father, and we still don't, but she left clues."

"Like what?"

"Mom always had a fear that no one would show up at her funeral and doubted they would fill a back-row pew in a small church."

"How does something like that get worked into a conversation?"

"I suppose she might have said it in jest. But what I know, and in my heart, I believe she was asking for help, and nobody was listening."

Clair could tell he was tearing up and upset.

"I remember like it was yesterday. The chapel was filled to capacity. Who'd have thought? Obviously not her."

Clair had never seen this side of him before and reached over and touched his hand.

"I'm so sorry, Glenn."

He said nothing and shook his head.

"I don't get it. Like my mother and I suppose many others, including you, too often suicide seems to be a rational solution to complex issues. Mom didn't drink or use drugs we know of. But this I know. When you combine depression with drugs, alcohol, physical and emotional abuse, it's like a bad math equation, and you are the sum of it."

Clair didn't look at him, and with shame in her voice, said, "I guess you're a little disappointed."

"Disappointed is an understatement, I'm afraid for you."

"Afraid of what?"

He didn't pull any punches.

"I fear the next time you might be successful, and I can assure you, there will be a next time."

She glared at him, and said, "Why would you say such a thing?"

"Because it's true. It's in your DNA. Do you know who the real demons are?"

Without an answer, he continued.

"I'll tell you who they are; they're more of a what than a who. It's that shit scattered all over your bedroom and everything else you used to try to kill yourself with."

Then shouted, "There are your fucking demons!"

Clair was speechless, but he was right.

Glenn was still angry and any professionalism he had left in him, was now a forgone conclusion.

"Clair, you have been a client of mine for some time now, and I've gotten to know you. I care about you and your well-being, but you make me question things. I have asked myself a thousand times why does someone want to die more than they want to live? For the ones who were successful, the question remains unanswered. There are teams of researchers doing studies and tests all the time, and still no answers."

"Why?"

"Why do you think? Because it's a little hard to do a study with dead people. They aren't as cooperative as the living ones."

Glenn continued his rant and said those who failed a suicide, at least a few clues of the "why's" are answered.

"Let's go for a ride; I want to show you something."

After a silent, tedious walk down the corridors of the building, they got to his car and climbed in.

With nervous curiosity, Clair asked, "Where are we going?"

Glenn slammed the car door and said, "You'll know when we get there."

It took forty minutes to get to this mysterious location with no further conversation. While he drove, Glenn stared straight out toward the road and took the time to deliver an unwanted speech.

"There are four ways to die I know of."

He used his fingers as a counter.

"Number one —natural death."

Then added his middle finger.

"Two —murder," then added to the chorus… his ring finger. "Three —accident."

And finally, the smallest of his digits complimented the others.

"Last, but not least —suicide. You seem to have mastered half of them. If you can think of anything else, I'm all ears."

The last few miles were driven with more silence.

They arrived at a large, single-story building outside of town. Several cars filled the parking lot. She had to squint her eyes to read the sign at its entrance. It was The Garrard Learning Center named after its founder, Dr. Vandergriff Garrard. It was a school and housed the most severe mentally and physically challenged children, teens, and young adults.

"Why are you taking me to this place?"

When in a therapeutic setting, and with little emotion, Glenn used a barrage of open-ended questions he learned in counselor training, such as, "Why do you feel that way?" and "Why do you think that is?" Today would be much different.

While still in the car, he turned to her stating frankly, "I'm throwing the therapy handbook out the window."

She thought to herself, "*Uh-oh.*"

His usual calm tone pivoted.

"You think your life is so fucked up? I'll show you fucked up."

He was right about one thing; he tossed the handbook out the window. Clair never heard Glenn talk like that before. They got out, and again he slammed the car door.

"You're awfully tough on car doors."

"Not now, Clair. I'm not in the mood."

At a faster pace, he made his way to the front door first. She arrived a couple of seconds later. He rang the buzzer and a voice through the speaker answered.

"May I help you?"

"Hi, I'm Glenn Bayer, we're here to see Stanley."

The security lock clicked, he opened the door, and motioned toward its entrance, said, "After you."

Clair walked in ahead of him. Now they were side-by-side. Glenn was only a step away from her when the administrator, Dr. Debbie Ellison came down the stretch of the hallway and greeted them. She extended her hand and clasped his.

"Good to see you."

"You too, Debbie. This is my friend, Clair, who I mentioned earlier."

Clair was nervous and reluctant but extended her hand.

Dr. Ellison shook Clair's hand and said all the while, "Very pleased to meet you."

"Me too," and thought, "*She has the grip of a corrupt politician.*"

Not visible to the other two, when Debbie released her hand, Clair shook it a little to ease the pain.

"I guess you're here to see Stanley. He's excited to see you. It's been a while."

He remained as professional as he could, but, somewhat ashamed, replied, "I know."

The trio made their way to the gym where many of the clients and patients were busy with exercise or other physical activity within their limits. On the way, Dr. Ellison wanted to show them a piece of equipment that had been donated. She was so excited about it; you would have thought she had won a new car.

At the gym, a lot of noises filled the air. It was brightly lit, chilly, and to Clair, it smelled the same as her high school gymnasium; like stale jockey straps from the boy's locker room. Here, it was the smell of dirty diapers and underwear.

The bleachers rattled as some of the kids were stomping on them cheering for the players in a wheelchair basketball game. Age and gender made no difference in this place; they were one and the same. Stanley noticed Glenn from across the court and motored his way toward him in his wheelchair. He used his right hand to maneuver his chair; with the other one, weak and uncontrollable, he waved to Glenn.

All you could hear coming from him was a distorted, "*Hi Gen! Hi Gen! Hi Gen!*"

Gen was as close as he could get to saying Glenn's name. They met near the water cooler, and he struggled to reach for him with his arms. The two embraced, and Stanley's arms flopped on Glenn's back trying to hug and pat him, and Glenn returned the patting with gentler little ones.

"*I wuv you, Gen.*"

They stopped embracing, and he said, "Me too, Stanley. I want you to meet a friend of mine. This is Clair."

Stanley was shy, and with his head lowered, peeked up enough to get a look at her.

"*Hi, Cwair, gu… gu… good to me… me… meet you.*"

'Cwair' was also the best he could do to pronounce her name.

"Clair, I'd like you to meet my brother, Stanley."

She looked at Glenn with a confused expression, then said, "Your brother?"

Stanley tapped on his arm.

"*Come heah, I wa... wa... want to ta... talk to you.*"

He leaned in close and whispered, "*She's pwetty.*"

Glenn moved away from him, looked at her then back at him.

"You think so?"

Clair overheard the conversation and his sarcastic reply and punched him on the arm.

Taken aback by her gentle assault, he added, "You're right. She's a regular Miss America."

Clair grinned.

"That's better."

Stanley laughed as he spoke.

Not in his usual style and with a hint of sarcasm, he asked, "*Is she your gurrrrlfend?*"

He flapped both arms, laughing the whole time.

"No, she is not my girlfriend."

He stopped with the flailing arms and said, "*You sa... sa... said she was yur fend, and she is a gurl, so that makes her yur gurlfend!*"

He laughed again and pounded his thighs like a snare drum. They all shared a laugh, and Clair began to relax.

The three got control over themselves, and Glenn pulled out a clean handkerchief from his pocket. He motioned for Stanley to sit still and tried not to shake. He wobbled a little, but Glenn's light touch held his chin steady as he wiped away some drool that trickled down from his mouth.

"Can Clair and I walk around with you for a little while.?"

"Hell ya!"

"Boy, you got that out loud and clear."

As they were moving along, Stanley asked, "*Guess what, Cwair?*"

"What is it?"

"*I didn't fawt in gwoop today.*"

"That's good, Stanley."

Confused at what to say, she raised both arms and looked at Glenn with an expression that asked, 'now what?' He smiled and with a nodded twitch toward Stanley, prompted her to say something. She got the hint and returned the nod.

Then in gentle, little circling motions, rubbed him on the back, and said, "I'm proud of you. I'm sure everyone appreciated your courtesy."

"*Thank you, Cwair.*"

They wandered around for a while, and as they did, Clair was watching many of the kids, sometimes in amazement and other times in astonishment. In another room down the hallway, some of them lay on padded cushions on the floor and squirmed around like a newborn child while others moaned or cried. Some were strapped to a wheelchair so they wouldn't fall off. There were a few who sat motionless, just gazing into space. Clair witnessed several of them getting their much-needed medication to either prolong their lives or maintain it.

She was noticeably upset by the experience and everything around her.

Wiping moistened eyes, Clair said, "I hope this isn't one of your date, hot spots."

"I've brought one of them along to meet him."

"How'd that go?"

"There wasn't a next one. This visit is different. It is for you. Like I said earlier, the handbook got tossed out when I showed you this place. This might help with a better understanding of yourself."

In a curt tone, she said, "Well, it's working. Thanks."

"Before we go, take a hard look around. I want you to see what condition they are in and gaze into their faces."

Clair zoomed in on several and surveyed each of them with focused eyes.

"I feel terrible. Those poor kids."

"You know what? This is as good as it gets for most of them, including Stanley."

Looking at Glenn, she teared up again.

"Why are you doing this?"

Quiet and uncontrollable sobbing came from her when she asked and demanded an answer.

"I'm not doing anything to you. This is their reality. You think there isn't a kid in this place that wouldn't trade you for your self-loathing, pathetic set of circumstances?"

"That's not fair!"

"Fair?" he exclaimed.

Then pointing, said, "Ask them what's fair. To them, 'fair' is a place they go to every once in a while, play a few games, see an elephant and maybe eat cotton candy if they can hold it in their stomach long enough to enjoy it. A meal for many of them is a tube shoved in their gut with a mixture of a vitamin-infused muck to keep them nourished, and Stanley is one of them."

Glenn continued the lecture.

"Some struggle to live, like those around us, while others fight to die. Here's the deal. You have a choice most of these people don't. Did you ever consider a fate worse than death? A lot of it is right in front of you. Too many of these and their families, death would be a welcomed friend."

She did not like hearing any of this but paid attention to every word.

"Clair, this is the most unprofessional thing I could ever say to you, but if you don't pull your head out of your ass, you could end up in the adult version of this if you fail to kill yourself again. Want to see one? It's next door."

"No. I've seen enough."

Clair looked up and took a quick glance at Glenn, then he began walking away and said, "We have to get out of here."

She caught up with him, and said their goodbyes to Stanley and Dr. Ellison then retreated to the car. The drive to her apartment was silent. Neither of them spoke and sat there for several minutes. Clair turned toward Glenn.

"I like your brother. What's wrong with him?"

He let out a deep sigh.

"You already know he has Downs Syndrome, and to further complicate his life, he gets to add amyotrophic lateral sclerosis to the list."

She had never heard of that before and tried to repeat him but struggled. "What is ah... me... yo... tro... fick?"

"In laymen terms, Lou Gehrig's Disease. Downs hardly kills, but ALS is fatal. He was diagnosed three years ago when he was eighteen. It is rare for a teenager or a younger person to contract it, and time is not his friend."

Clair turned away and stared out the window.

"How much time?"

"Let me say it this way; whenever I get a call from the center, my heart skips a beat."

They arrived at her apartment, but before he dropped her off, he had one last thing to say to recap the day.

"You have it in you to change and accept the things you can't."

Scratching her head, she said, "That sounds familiar."

"It should. I'm paraphrasing. You see, Clair, the past is what haunts us. The present is where we find the truth and healing begins. The future holds the prize for that truth and healing, but it takes hard work and a strong commitment. You met those things that haunted you straight on. There is not a therapist, treatment center, pill or magic potion on the planet that can do that for you. What we can do, is guide you through the journey and help you see the light at the other end of a tunnel. Now take what you have learned, go out in the world and live in it."

Clair let out a giggle.

"Up to now, that light at the end of it was a train."

Glenn's response was quick.

"Find another tunnel."

Clair made several trips to see her new friend. They shared many hours together over a four-month span of time. Stanley taught her how to play Texas Hold'em —the poker game. But his favorite was the board game Mouse Trap. One of the staff members approached her one day and told her how much Stanley liked her, even referring to her as his girlfriend. It made her smile.

On one of her visits, and out of the blue, he asked if she believed in God.

"I think so."

"*Do you bewieve in baby Jesus?*"

Not knowing how to answer, placated him instead.

"Yes, I believe in baby Jesus."

Clair walked the hallways with him for a while. After a few hours, he said he was tired.

"Do you want to go to sleep?"

"*Yeah. Will you tu... tu... tuck me in?*"

They got to his dorm room, and with the help from an aide, they lifted him from his wheelchair and placed him in his bed. Before the aide left, she told him it was his feeding time. He ordered a steak and potatoes.

She smiled at him and said, "Sure thing, Stanley, coming right up."

A few minutes later she returned with tubes and a bottle of the sludge Glenn had mentioned.

"I'll set these here until you are ready."

Clair looked at the cart with his "dinner."

He glanced at her, then checked out the tray and said, "*Yummy. Wa... wa... want some?*"

They spent several more minutes together during his feeding.

"*Isn't this neato? I can ta... ta... talk and e... e... eat at the same time.*"

His comment left her speechless, but it was his sense of humor and his way of making her feel at ease.

The aide came back to the room and removed the feeding tube.

"*Tell the cu... cu... cook, thanks.*"

"Will do. Sleep tight."

"*D... d... don't le... le... let the bed bu... bugs bite.*"

The aide smiled.

"Good night."

It was close to his bedtime. Clair pulled the blanket from the foot of the bed and covered him. He reached for her hand.

"*Cwair, I want you to bewieve in God.*"

He had been somber but perked up.

"*I'm going to Heaven and play with baby Jesus.*"

"That's sweet."

"*A nice wady said when I go to Heaven, I'll be normal again.*"

"Stanley, she might be a nice lady, but you, my friend, are the most normal person I know, and I know a few crazies."

He laughed.

"*Yuah funny, Cwair.*"

He settled on the pillow and wiggled around a little to get comfortable. Once relaxed, he tilted his head and looked at her.

He took a labored breath and said, "*I la... la... luuuv you, Cu-laaair.*"

"Very good, Stanley. You're ready to give a speech."

"*I ha... ha... have, be... been pwacticing.*"

"Well it sure paid off. I love you too."

Stanley couldn't see the tears forming or get the sense of the love replacing the anger in Clair's heart. She kissed him on the cheek and gave a light tap on the chest.

"I'll see you in a day or two."

And she did.

Stanley was a simple educator and taught Clair a few life lessons. One of them was not to be afraid and be happy. He never said those things, but the way he lived spoke volumes with his actions and attitude.

With continued counseling and after meeting Stanley, Clair knew there were options. She could go down the same path that was killing her, or get fixed, and wanted to prove everyone wrong betting against her, including Glenn. Now the cards were in her hands.

"Live one day at a time" is a cute saying, but for Stanley, each new one was precious because his life was a day-to-day struggle. Clair had choices to make. His ran out years ago, and he knew it. Stanley treated every day as a gift and lived each one to its fullest. He never complained, always smiled, and was happy in the purest sense. He helped his friends in worse shape than he was... and there weren't many. His life was simple and honest. He only wanted love and to be loved and not much more.

A few weeks later, she went to see Stanley, and Glenn was there. His eyes were red and swollen and included an expressionless look on his face. Clair could tell that he had been crying.

"What is it, Glenn?"

Now in a panic, asked, "Where is Stanley?"

Glenn shook his head, and with both arms, he flung them around her and held tight then whispered, "Stanley died this morning. He asked for you."

She held him even tighter and tried her best to keep her emotions. This was new to Clair, and had feelings that were exploding deep in her soul, but also knew it was time to comfort Glenn — hers would have to wait.

Chapter XIV

Clair drove to a nearby secluded park and sat there for several hours. Her hands gripped the steering wheel with so much force it left an indentation. She never moved a muscle and stared out straight in front; the view didn't even register. This went on until almost dark.

The few times Clair shifted position, was only because of a brief distraction when people came and went during her stay, then only glanced for a second or two. She saw a family picnicking, playing around, and having fun. There were also two young lovers kissing and leaning against a tall oak tree and several neighborhood kids assembled for a make-shift soccer game. As a witness to all the activity, she never made a sound and kept staring.

It was dark by now, and the park was void of any people, except for her. What little light there was, came as a courtesy of a full moon and millions of stars twinkling on a cloudless night sky. She interrupted her silence and got out. She stumbled around like a zombie for a few yards, stopped in place, and fell like a rag doll to her knees. Still silent, but using both fists, leaned forward to pound the ground so hard, her hands and knuckles bled. She was huffing and puffing, and the only sound was her primal moans and groans. Drained of strength, she stopped pounding, raised both clenched fists in the air, and screamed with so much force it hurt her. The pain felt like she'd been hit in the gut with a baseball bat.

Completely spent, her face soaked in tears and sweat, looked up toward the heavens and yelled, "Why? Why? Why?"

The questions bounced off the trees and raced toward the heavenly sky.

"He did nothing to you! He didn't do anything to anybody!"

Clair was getting it, and rightly so; Stanley didn't do anything, and for the first time she understood. His death and her abuse were neither one's fault. Even with some clarity, it did not diminish her anger. She dropped again to the ground on bent knees. Covering her face with her hands, a flood of tears mixed with blood flowed through her fingers while she sobbed.

Toward the end, Clair raised herself from the ground, paused, looked up, and screamed, "Fuck you!"

Tired and exhausted, she collapsed. Her face lay in the dirt, and grass clippings stuck in her hair. The thought of eternal damnation for cursing God put fear in her heart. At that moment, allowing herself to feel was more important than salvation. Salvation could be restored, Stanley's life could not. Perhaps God already understood.

With less anger but increased sobbing, got up to her knees, again looked toward the sky and whispered, "I hate you."

Chapter XV

The death of her young friend seemed enough of an excuse for at least a drink or two… or several. A week later she went to Sid's, but bypassed McDonald's. Clair took her usual stroll as before. Along the way, glanced up at the billboard and noticed it was a new one.

"It took you long enough."

Clair got to the front entrance, stared at the flashing open sign, turned, and walked away.

Finally recognizing what the demon was, gave her some amount of tranquility, but remained reserved. Stanley's death and more answers of 'why' hit her hard. Glenn tried to explain her sorrow, any regrets and what it meant. He also had regret in his own life and wasn't sure why… yet. Glenn hurt too, but wanted to help Clair understand her sadness, and it helped him too. They met at his office for a scheduled private, one-on-one session.

She tapped on his half-opened office door.

Looking at his watch, he said, "Hi, Clair, right on time. Come in and take a seat."

He was sitting at his desk and jotted down a few last-minute notes from an earlier session. He turned and swung a side chair around close to his. They faced each other, almost an arm's length away.

"Let's get started. You and I have spent plenty of time together, and I must say, you have come a long way. I will not use a lot of psychobabble, and I'm way out of my pay-grade. I know a little about this stuff, did some research, and the rest, well, to be honest, I'm just going to wing it. So, let's cut to the chase."

She settled back in the chair.

"I'm listening."

Glenn cleared his throat and began.

"Stanley's death took something away from you, and it makes sense you might feel the way you do. You found something you'd never known growing up: trust, a good relationship, and bonding, all those things you never experienced as a child. They were theories and did not exist for someone who has gone through what you did. Then Stanley came along. He changed that and provided all three."

"That makes sense."

During the conversation, she didn't move a muscle. Glenn noticed her eyes shed a tear or two and reached into a lower drawer for a tissue. He handed it to her, and she placed it in her lap.

"Thanks."

"You're welcome. We buy them by the truckload."

That put a smile on her face.

"Go on, you're on a roll."

Glenn turned away and took a few notes. Almost moving to the edge of the seat, Clair tried to maneuver her way around him to see what he was jotting down. He swung around, and she snapped back into her previous position, hoping he didn't notice her spying.

"Now where was I?"

Clair was about to help him out, and he put up his hand to stop her.

"Excuse me a sec."

He turned back to his notes and stayed focused on them.

He never looked up, kept writing, then said matter-of-factly, "I think you feel responsible for his death."

"I don't understand."

He finished his note with a dotted I and a crossed T. Afterward, he spun his chair around and gave her his attention.

"We in the 'biz' sometimes throw the term 'magical thinking' around. Some feel they can hope or pray for impossible things to go away or not let happen. If the scenario had turned to the worst, they wished it was you instead of them. But I think what you are experiencing is survivor's guilt."

"I don't get it."

"The term originated from war. When a fellow soldier died, and the other didn't they felt guilty. You and Stanley also had your own battles. His was physical, and yours emotional. You two were comrades in arms, so-to-speak, and the feelings you had toward him reinforced guilt. To add to it, after Stanley passed, it strengthened your feeling you were undeserving of anything worthwhile in your life. You allowed yourself to love and trust someone, perhaps for the first time. You let your guard down long enough and invited someone else in."

There was evidence of a slight sniffle, and with the tissue still in her grasp, took a second to blow her nose.

Glenn knew he was getting close to something and didn't want her to quit.

"Are you all right? Is this too much for now?"

"I'm soaking it in."

A single tear flowed, and she wiped it hoping Glenn didn't notice. Clair had been leaning forward, but now sat straight up in the chair. With her back against it, had a sense she wasn't going to like what was coming. Her legs were crossed, and her arms lay loosely over her chest, but they were tightening with every word he spoke.

"This is a stretch, but I believe you feel responsible for his death or perhaps envious that it was him and not you."

"You're right, that was a stretch, but I'm dying to know what you're talking about."

"I'll try to explain it."

"Please do."

"Here it goes. The love you had for him was sabotaged by his death because you were unworthy of it. It was new territory for you. Now, here comes the 'wing it' part, but I believe I'm right. To use the expression, 'if it weren't for bad luck, I'd have no luck at all.' You may have felt like the rough times in your life contributed to his death, and his death affirmed those feelings. Now, you and I both know it isn't true, at least not in our head, but sometimes our heart needs to catch up."

"What about envy?"

"He's dead, and you're not. His suffering ended."

Clair looked away and ignored him, reached for the tissue drawer, pulled out a handful and cried.

"He trusted me, and I let him die."

This went on for a minute or two, and Glenn let her take as much time as she needed.

Clair reached for another tissue from the stockpile and tossed the spent ones into a wastebasket several feet away. Glenn followed its path in the air.

"Nice shot."

She smiled and blew her nose again.

Glenn redirected the conversation.

"Listen to what I am saying."

He moved closer, placed both hands on her shoulders, and looked her right in the eyes.

"You are not responsible for his death. The disease killed him, and there was nothing anyone could do."

With not much else to say, she whispered, "I do wish it was me instead of him."

"I don't. Stanley's was inevitable; you still have a chance, and one other thing…"

"What?" she asked while still sobbing.

"… God didn't do it either."

"I guess so. We've already had a chat."

"Me too. I thanked Him for giving us Stanley and was grateful for the time we had together. How was yours?"

"Not as good. We're not on speaking terms at the moment."

"That's between you and Him."

She blew her nose one last time and again tossed the tissue toward the wastebasket. This time, it didn't hit its target. She watched as it bounced off the rim and fell to the floor.

"Figures."

Glenn got up, walked a few steps away and placed the tissue in the trash with the others. Returning to his chair, Clair covered her face with her hands and wept.

"I miss him so much."

"Me too, Clair, every day. The bottom line is, he loved and trusted you, but what's more important, is that you loved and trusted him. You may not know it now, but that's a biggie. I want to ask you a question."

"Fire away."

Glenn sat back in his chair and asked, "What do you think depression is? Describe it."

Clair paused for a moment.

"That's easy. Sometimes I felt that my back was against the wall, and it was tall and wide and no way to escape its grasp. It was like an emotional glue that kept me stuck to it."

Glenn was obviously impressed.

"Pretty good. What about now?"

"The wall is smaller."

They had a few moments together though not much was said. It was apparent neither one had much going on, and both of them took a few minutes to relax. It was casual and quiet except for a squeaky ceiling fan. During the silence, she reached into her purse for some lip gloss and did her nails; he picked up a magazine and flipped its pages. Glenn stopped on one of the pages.

"Huh."

Then said aloud, "You can't hide the smell; all you do is mask the odor."

"What on God's green earth does that mean?"

"It's right here. See?"

He showed the page, and she glanced at it.

"It's a room freshener ad, but it got me to thinking about you."

"Gee whiz, thanks a lot."

"You misunderstood me. I think a lot of the time, people put on a mask to survive and hide, but under the surface of it lies a deeper cause of why they need one. For once, you lifted yours enough to let some of us take a peek —" then pointing at her heart — "who Clair really is."

"I thought you were off the clock."

Glenn tossed the magazine back on his desk.

"I was. I have another client in the waiting room, so let's wrap it up. Do you have any questions?"

"No, I don't think so. I'm good."

"How are the meds?"

"Peachy keen."

He gave her a light pat on the knee.

"Alrighty then. Godspeed and keep up the good work. Call anytime."

Glenn worked on his notes as she went toward the door.

"Clair?"

She stopped and turned.

"Yes, Glenn, what is it?"

He never looked up from his note-taking and spoke as he wrote.

"I want you to know how proud I am of you."

She said nothing, smiled, and continued to walk out.

"One more thing."

Again, she turned.

"What?"

"You've inspired me to write a book why people kill themselves."

"Splendid. What's it called."

"Why People Kill Themselves."

She laughed.

"Very original."

Now it was her turn.

"Glenn?"

Still looking at her, he responded.

"Yes?"

"You make me smile."

He smiled in return.

That was her last visit with Glenn. He signed off on the chart using the typical counseling shorthand and symbols, but translated it read: "Treatment plan complete, goals at level. Send final bill."

At the end of his notes, one statement was highlighted with a yellow marker. It read:

"Affect, normal," meaning she was doing just fine. For once, it was the truth and not an acronym.

* * *

Clair remembered to stop by her mother's house for some old art supplies stored in the attic. Clair arrived at the house and noticed her mother's car wasn't there. She knocked on the back door and let herself in.

She hadn't paid too much attention but heard a noise coming from the kitchen. Clair stuck her head around the corner to get a look. It was Edward.

He was eating cereal, and between bites, said, "Hello, Clair. You look lovely."

She ignored him, and he went back to maul the rest of his meal.

As Edward wiped milk dripping running down the side of his mouth, and asked, "What are you doing here?"

"I'm here to pick up a few things."

"Do you want any help?" he asked with a smirk on his face.

"No thanks, I can do it myself."

She made her way to the hallway a few feet from where her bedroom used to be and pulled the rope to let down the ceiling ladder. Placing one foot on the first rung and the other flat on the floor, glanced down the hallway which led to her old bedroom. Clair could still see the scratches and indentions left behind on the door frame from the times Edward tried to break into her room. Flashes of the past raced through her, and felt the need to get the hell out of there, but made the climb instead. At the top, within reach, she found the light switch and flipped it on. With both feet safely on the attic floor, she went to the other side where her stuff was stored. The boxes were stacked and labeled, then went through them one at a time.

Clair spent several minutes going through some old photos. Many of them brought back fond memories; some not so much. Two of them got her attention. The first one was of her father holding her in a white, christening gown when she was an infant. It put a smile on her face because her father looked happy and proud. The other confused her. It was a snapshot of her and Edward at a carnival. She was six, and he, twelve. It was a posed shot, and both wore cowboy outfits; Clair was mounted on top of a horse, and Edward held its reins. The memory ran through her mind, and for a moment thought it was cute.

She rummaged through a few more boxes and came across something.

"What do we have here?"

She removed a piece of construction paper. It had been folded multiple times down from a full sheet to one small enough to carry in her pocket. Clair unfolded the brittle piece of paper and found a crayon drawing. The background was familiar.

"I remember this. It's been a while."

The drawing was a little girl, adorned with long, dark hair, holding a stuffed animal, sitting on a small rocking chair looking out a window. The stuffed toy had brown fur and a bow tie. Below the drawing were some printed words and read them aloud:

Once upon a time, there was a girl named Clair,
Who sat on her favorite chair with Teddy the bear.
She dreamed that one day a young prince would come and rescue her.
Clair wished and wished, and tried and tried,
But all that Clair had was Teddy the bear.
She held it tight and cried and cried.

A line in it caught her eye; the one about being saved by a prince and read the line again then said to herself, "That didn't work out so well, now did it?"

She looked at it one more time and ran her fingers over her art piece, almost caressing it.

"Pretty good for a kid."

She stared at it again, wadded it up into a tight ball, and threw it back in the box.

Clair remained preoccupied for a while longer, then felt a presence. She turned, and there stood Edward. The dim light showed the shadow of a face. Startled, she yelled at him.

"Dammit, Edward! You scared the crap out of me!"

"I wanted to help," he said in a sheepish tone.

"And I told you I needed none."

Clair turned away from him and toward the box. She stood there firm and confident, but trembled on the inside. She felt his eyes gawking her body.

With her back still turned, she said, "Why don't you go back downstairs and do whatever it was you were doing."

She looked through another box and tried to ignore him.

He wore a stained, smelly tank-top and clung to a rafter with both hands swaying back and forth.

"I'm in no hurry," he replied with a grin.

Again, ignored him and kept looking through the box.

As she gathered a few things, Edward said something inaudible, like, "Do you want to suck my...."

Clair turned toward him and glared.

"What did you say?"

"You heard me."

"You're right... I heard you. Guess what, Edward? Today is your lucky day. You're going to get your wish."

Still frightened, Clair approached and stopped in front of him. He was still suspended from the beam, and she slowly and seductively freed the top button of her blouse with her left hand and lightly brushed her breast with the other.

"Why don't you take off your pants."

His stench made her sick to her stomach but remained calm. He happily obeyed and wrestled with his belt, then unbuttoned his jeans to lower them. Clair seized the opportunity right before his pants slid down, then gathered all her strength and kicked him in the balls as hard as she could; so hard, it took his breath away and lifted him off the floor. When she did, it sounded like two church bells bellowing out their chimes of freedom throughout the city, but it was more of a loud clunk. Nonetheless, it was effective. The pain shot throughout his entire body, and in an instant, fell to the floor screaming.

Edward tucked his knees toward his chest in a fetal position and covered his injured groin with both hands, protecting them from another onslaught. Clair kneeled beside him, forced his hands aside, grabbed his crotch and squeezed as hard as she could. He yelled in agony, and the louder he got, the harder she clamped down. Above his loud moans, she got nose to nose and said with the sternest of warnings.

"If you ever touch me or say anything stupid again, the next time I'll shoot those things off! Capiche?"

He couldn't move and still moaned and gasped for breath. He tried to wrestle free, and when he did, the noose around "the boys" got stronger.

"Well? I'm waiting for an answer."

All he could say, was, "Go to hell."

Clair released him and replied, "I've already been there."

She got to her feet and dealt him a final kick to the face, then gathered her things and left him alone in the attic, turned off the light and locked the ceiling door behind. Before leaving, she pulled the wadded piece of paper out of the box, reshaped it, and placed it in her pocket, back where it belonged.

"I have a question, Edward. Who did to you, what you did to me all those years?"

He was still moaning and groaning on the floor but managed an answer.

"Who didn't?"

She wasn't sympathetic, but offered a piece of final advice.

"I suggest you get a therapist, and while you're at it, find a good urologist. From the looks of things, you'll need one."

She got to the front door, put her things down and made a makeshift bullhorn with her hands, shouting loud and clear.

"I hope you like rats!"

Outside, near the driveway, she heard him pounding on the ceiling attic door, but this time, they were pleas instead of demands like before.

"Clair, open the damn door! Please!"

His words were followed by more pounding. For the first time, she could walk away from the pounding and not be afraid and sang and whistled all the way to her apartment. She unloaded the box, hauled them inside, and worked on her next masterpiece. After several hours of solitude, Edward freed himself, took her advice and left her alone. They never spoke again. To this day, he still walks with a limp.

* * *

Clair made a few new friends and discarded many. Edward also received counseling, but not the way you might expect. Some states in the U.S do not have a statute of limitations for sexual assault of a child, and Clair's was one of them. Oops. Years later, several of Edward's victims filed a criminal complaint, but there were others who didn't because of the embarrassment. Clair was among the group that chose not to testify, but the bravest did. The charges were investigated, he was indicted and went to trial and found guilty of most of the accusations. The list was narrowed down to the ten most severe cases, and he was convicted on all of them. In a plea deal before trial, the best his lawyer could get was ten ninety-nine-year terms in the penitentiary, but if he behaves himself, he'll get out at the tender age of ninety-five.

Clair heard while in prison, Edward got married. He had always been scrawny as a kid and into adulthood. He stood at five foot eight and was very thin, almost frail in stature. His wife's name was Bubba. They were cellmates, and I suppose dating wasn't enough, so they tied the knot —at Bubba's request. His bride was much taller than Edward. He was a six-foot-four-inch, two hundred forty-pound transvestite. Bubba loved dressing up as a ballerina, and a lifelong dream was to wear a tutu at "her" wedding — and did. The only photo Clair ever saw of the newlyweds was the one when Bubba cradled Edward like an infant. Bubba was all smiles; Edward's expression was that of terror.

Chapter XVI

It had been five years since Stanley's death. Since then, Clair's life had gone full circle, discovering how and why to live. Though he never knew, Stanley helped lead and guide her down that pathway.

At thirty-three years old, her art career took off. Her exhibits had become quite popular around the country, including many museums in Europe.

She tamed her demon, and with a bit of humor told herself, "Except for that damn ape!"

The gorilla experiment at the museum had been her motivation ever since. The piece that put her on the map was a watercolor painting of a beautiful lady pushing a young man in a wheelchair through a grassy meadow.

"I guess it spoke to them."

She was working on a new project and was interrupted by a phone call.

"Hello."

"Hi, Clair, it's me."

Right away, she recognized the voice.

"Hunter?"

"Yeah, it's me. How have you been?"

"Great! It's good to hear from you. What's new?"

She placed her brush on the easel, then paced back and forth as far as the phone cord would allow.

"Going well. I'm working for Dad full time and going to give a stab at college again and start over."

More relaxed by now, she giggled, "Start over? You went for one day."

He laughed, "I have to re-enroll you know and go through that paperwork nightmare."

"I'm proud of you. Are you staying straight?"

Hunter replied, "Clean as a whistle. I haven't touched a thing for over two years."

"Well, ditto on being proud again."

"It was hard at first, but I went to meetings and stayed after it. I had to start over a few times —I have a box full of relapse chips to prove it."

They both got a laugh, then he asked, "You?"

"You, what?"

"Are you, I mean have you..."

Clair interrupted, "Tried to slit my wrists?"

"Yeah, that."

"You can say it Hunter; it won't kill you."

There was more laughter from the two.

"Hunter, I'm doing fine —and don't say it or think it," referring to the FINE acronym.

"I won't say a word."

She couldn't see, but envisioned him gesturing the zippering of his mouth. They chatted for what seemed like hours, catching up on things since they broke up.

It had been lighthearted up to this point, then he changed the tone.

"I suppose you heard about Troy."

The conversation went silent for a moment.

"Yes, I did. Why didn't you go to the funeral?"

"Just couldn't. It was me who found the body."

Clair said nothing and stayed with him. She could hear in his voice he was getting a little shaky.

"I went to his house to pick him up as usual. He was going to get his ninety-day chip for staying clean. Clair, it was the most horrible thing

I'd ever seen. When I saw him, I couldn't breathe. He didn't fool around either. I don't know what kind of bullet he used, but it blew half of his head off! It took two days to clean up his bedroom. The coroner said he'd been dead somewhere between twenty-four and thirty-six hours."

With the phone in one hand, he rested his cheek on the other and sobbed.

"I still can't get the smell out of my mind."

"That's terrible, Hunter. I never knew it was you who found him."

Clair heard the rustling of tissue paper and his sniffles.

"The family wanted me to help with the arrangements and the funeral director suggested a closed casket service was in order because there was too much damage to make Troy presentable."

Clair could hear in Hunter's voice the pain and sorrow he was experiencing.

"He was one of my best friends."

His sobbing continued.

"I wish he would have said something. I could have helped him."

"Hunter, sweetie, there was nothing you could do."

"You're right."

His sadness turned to a hint of anger.

"But don't they realize what they do to us?"

Clair replied, "It's more complicated than that."

He talked for several more minutes, and she continued to listen. For once in her lifetime, got a firsthand account of the aftermath that goes along with a suicide the victim will never see or hear.

Hunter was gasping for words.

"I liked him a lot."

"Me too. You okay?"

Still sniffling, but more calm, replied, "No, I'm not."

"Time will heal."

"Does it?"

Clair stayed on the phone with Hunter, giving him much needed comfort. He regained control of himself long enough to finish their talk.

"Before I go, there's one more thing."

"What is it?"

"I met a girl."

There was more brief silence at both ends of the line. Hunter was waiting for a response, and Clair was thinking about what to say. In her heart, she knew the two were not a match, and they'd go nowhere together. Hunter and Clair were two lost souls who ran into each other at a time and place when they needed it the most.

"Are you still there?" Hunter asked.

"Yes, I am. I'm happy for you, both of you."

"Thanks, that means a lot. I gotta scoot, I'm having a meeting with the managers at the car wash in an hour. Gotta fire one of them for handing out free car washes to friends."

"You have fun with that."

"You know I will."

Hunter stalled for a moment.

"I will always love you," he said with a little break in his voice.

She thought about his words and didn't respond to them.

"I hope you have a great life. We had a lot of laughs. I gotta go too. Bye now."

She hung up the phone, sat on the chair nearby, twirled a strand of hair and smiled.

Moistened eyes followed her smile, and then whispered to herself, "I love you too, Hunter."

They spoke little afterward, but ran into each other occasionally. Hunter's life continued to prosper, and he picked up where he left off at school. He had experience with the first day; it was the second one that was new beginning. Hunter graduated with a teaching degree. He married the one he told Clair about and had two kids; a boy, Hunter junior, and a girl, Clarice.

* * *

Though Rae had never been formally introduced to Glenn, and he had only met her once or twice, two weeks later after Clair's final visit with him, convinced her mother to find a counselor. Glenn helped find a good one and referred her to one of his colleagues at another facility. Months passed, and Clair had one last visit with her mother, then cut ties for the next four years.

On a quiet day, Clair was at home doing much of nothing relaxing. She went off into her own little world and dozed off until a faint knock on the door woke her. Startled and half awake, got up, stumbled around, tripped over something, and almost fell getting to the door. She opened it, and to her surprise, it was her mother.

She stood there and asked, "Are you drunk?"

Clair thought that was a rude way to start a chat after such a long time, but kept it civil.

"No, Rae, I fell asleep, and you woke me. I nearly killed myself getting to the damn door! And, no, I'm not drunk. I might have a fractured leg though! I don't drink anymore and haven't for some time. What about you?"

Her mother said nothing and just stood there. Rae removed her sunglasses and Clair did a quick scan. She wore a stunning, baby blue dress with a matching scarf wrapped around her neck, all crowned with a stylish hat. Her hair and makeup were perfect, and for a moment, thought she was staring at Jackie O. Clair was stunned to see her and surprised at how great she looked.

"It's good to see you. May I come in? And by the way, its mother to you."

In a condescending tone, she apologized.

"Sorry, I'll keep it in mind."

Clair backed away from the door, and with a non-apologetic sweeping motion of her hand, asked her in, and led the way.

"I must warn you, the apartment is a mess."

She straightened magazines on an already cluttered coffee table, stacked them, and wiped the dust from the top one.

Rae walked in like a model on a runway. She looked all around, up and down with the eyes of an inspector and removed her hat.

"Clair, your apartment looks charming."

"I've been neglecting it a little. I've been busy."

"It looks hunky-dory."

Stunned, Clair looked at her.

"Do you know, Glenn?"

"Who's Glenn?"

"Never mind."

Clair went to the couch, fluffed the pillows, and told her to make herself at home. Rae sat and placed a pillow on her lap like a baby kitten.

"Do you want some hot tea or coffee?"

"I'll have a spot of tea."

Clair giggled.

"Spot of tea?"

"I'm dating a man from England, and that's what they say. Silly, isn't it?"

Shocked, Clair asked, "You're dating? How long?"

"Yes, to the first question, and four months to the second. Does it surprise you?"

"Well, kind of."

Her mother put the pillow to her face and took a whiff.

"You know what this smell reminds me of?"

"I don't know. Dirt?"

"No, it smells like you when you were a little girl, reminds me of your baby shampoo."

Rae took another long whiff, set the pillow aside, then gave herself a light tap on the knee.

"Now, how about that tea? Let me help."

"That's all right, you sit, and I'll get it together."

Clair went to the kitchen and Rae followed. Clair reached for the teapot, removed two cups from the cupboard, and turned on the burner.

"How do you like yours?"

"A little cream and sugar, please."

From the moment Clair opened the door until now, they hadn't gotten into an argument. She was amazed they were having a pleasant conversation —so far —and wondered when the bickering would begin. She filled the cups with hot water from the whistling kettle, along with a single tea bag each. They stood in the kitchen until it brewed and steeped. While they waited, more than tea was brewing.

"Clair, I want to talk to you."

"Oh boy, here we go."

Then braced herself. Clair could feel her neck tighten, and her heart pumped a little harder.

Slight defensiveness was in her voice, then asked, "What is it, *Moooom?*"

Rae ignored the sarcasm.

"Your father loved you very much."

Clair lightened up and thought, "*That wasn't too bad.*"

She dropped a cube of sugar for each, and stirred in a little cream for her mother, then handed over the cup.

"Be careful, it's hot—trust me. Let's go back to the living room and visit."

Once both settled in, her mother asked, "Did you hear what I said?"

"Yes, I did."

"Well?"

Clair snapped, "That's wonderful. You should put it in the paper."

It was still difficult to not be flippant with her mother.

Rae stayed calm and replied.

"Clair, you may know a lot of things, but you don't know everything."

Clair blew on her tea and listened.

"Your father was a kind and decent man. He worked hard to support us. I bet you never knew this, but when you were born, your dad was working two jobs and sold insurance at night."

"You're right... I didn't know."

"He also took care of his mother and sister. Both were disabled and lived together. He did all this and got his degree. His perseverance with the insurance company paid off, and he got a job at the corporate office."

Clair, in a white-flag-waving moment, said, "All I saw were the trappings of his success."

Rae reached for Clair's hand.

"It took a long time, but now I understand why you were angry with him."

Clair brushed her mother's hand aside, and with more condescension.

"Really?"

"Yes, really. I'll also let you in on something else. Your father was not aware of what Edward did to you, and neither did I until your friend's mother told me. I kept it from your dad because he had enough on his plate, so I handled it the only way I knew how. They don't teach that stuff in parent school. I was wrong how I treated you. I apologized once before, although not very heartfelt, I'm apologizing now,"— then placing her palm on her chest — "from my heart. Can you ever forgive me?"

Clair stared at her for a moment and saw her mother's eyes showing signs of a tear. Rae stared back waiting for a reply. Clair's eyes also moistened. She got up and took a seat next to her mom and placed a comforting arm around her.

"Mom, I forgave you way back then. I know it was a hard time for you. I didn't realize it until now."

Her mom started to cry.

"We had something special. I miss your father so much."

Rae continued to weep, and Clair continued to hold her.

"Maybe I'm the one who needs to apologize."

Her mother stopped crying and snapped at her.

And in the firmest of tones, said, "Now, you listen, Clair. You are a good girl and have nothing to apologize for."

She lowered her head and said, "I think the world owes you one."

Clair patted her mother on the leg and said, "Mom, I'm doing good, and have been for a while. I feel great. Better than ever."

She saw her mother's glances at her arms, but never got a close look.

"Honey, you have been a fighter since the day you were born, and I know for a fact you have had many battles. Did you ever win the war?"

Clair knew what she meant. She was wearing an artist's smock that covered most of her arms. To ease her curiosity, she pulled up her sleeves, turned them over, and showed clean, uncut, and healed scars. Clair displayed them like they were trophies. In a way, they were — but more so to Clair; they were a badge of honor.

She readjusted her sleeves, sliding them down the full length of her arm.

"I wish I knew more about Dad."

She ran her fingers through her hair and let out a forced breath.

"I missed out on a lot."

"So did your father, but every once in a while, he'd take you fishing. Do you remember?"

Clair folded her hands together and placed them under her chin, then rested her elbows on her knees. Her eyes wandered up and tried to recall the time. Rae sat and didn't say a word, then reached into her purse and pulled out an old photograph of Clair and her father. It was the two of them standing side-by-side with Clair holding up a small fish still on a hook. After a few moments, and studying the picture, a single tear ran down her face.

"I remember this."

Her mother again reached into her purse, this time for some tissue and gave it to Clair, keeping one for herself.

In a relaxed moment, Clair glanced at her purse and teased her.

"Do you have a car in that thing?"

"Lord knows I've got the room."

Clair dried the tear with hers and held it. Rae blew her nose, folded it and placed the tissue back in her purse.

"I do own a trashcan, mother."

"This is good; it's my excuse to get a new handbag."

Rae readjusted her seating and straightened her dress.

"Clair, I want you to know how proud I am of you."

"For what?"

"I read in the paper last month how wonderful your exhibit in New York was."

"Yeah, I cashed in on that one."

"It's not the money; it's about you. All the hell you went through growing up, and now, just look at you; all pretty and perky."

"I had a lot of help getting here, but thanks."

Almost like an unwarranted warning, Rae said, "I know this isn't very ladylike."

She blew her nose as loud as a fog horn, soiling another tissue. This time she shoved it between two sofa cushions instead of her purse.

"Sorry."

"No problem… it's just me. I'd rather it be the sofa instead of my shirt. That's my excuse to get a new sofa."

Between sniffles, her mother chuckled.

"You always had a sense of humor."

"I suppose so. Now tell me about this new boy you are seeing."

"His name is Thomas. Next to your father, he is the greatest man you'll ever meet. I think you'd like him."

"Mom, if he's good enough for you, he's good enough for me. Hell, maybe I should ask him out."

"You keep your paws off my boyfriend!"

Both had a big laugh.

"We spend a lot of time together. He lost his wife several years ago. Neither one of us dated until we met. He's a retired RAF pilot, and now he is a contractor with the Navy working as a flight simulator instructor for young pilots over in Pensacola."

"He sounds like a wonderful man. And yes, I'd like to meet him someday. Does he have a pension?"

"Clair! My word! I don't know about his business."

Rae leaned in close to her and said, "He ain't poor."

She sat up and continued.

"And it's getting serious. Thomas stays at my place quite a bit."

Seeming somewhat parental, Clair asked, "In separate rooms I assume?"

"Why of course."

Rae giggled like a teenage girl on prom night and said, "But we sneak around and meet in the guest bedroom."

The two laughed and couldn't stop.

"Oh my God, Mother! That's way too much information!"

Her mother got serious and said, "Don't worry, Clair, we just cuddle."

"I'll bet."

"Seriously, that's all we do."

In an instant, her mother jumped to her feet, threw both arms in the air, and said aloud, "Then we do it!"

"Mother!"

"Clair, I swear to God, he's a madman in the sack!"

"Enough already. I'm getting ready to throw up. Can we please change the subject?"

"Don't you do it?"

Clair glared at her mother right in the face and said, "Obviously not as much as others."

* * *

Clair and Rae spent many hours together for the next year, and it seemed neither one of them could let the other out of site. Rae invited Clair to her house one day. When she arrived, the coffee table was set with tea and cupcakes. They sat side-by-side and enjoyed the refreshments.

Clair licked the frosting clean from her cupcake, took a big bite and shoved the rest of it in her mouth.

"My God, Clair! Did you eat anything today?"

"Yeah, right before I came over."

Then grabbed another one.

"Mom, these are delicious! Can I have the recipe?"

Rae handed her an envelope.

"I've already got it ready for you."

"Thanks. So, what's the occasion? You want to go out?"

Her mother took a sip of tea and said, "No, Clair, I want to sit and visit with you."

Clair took the final bite of the second cupcake.

"OK. Whatever you want. Are there any more cupcakes?"

"Yes. I'll wrap the rest and send them with you."

Rae reached for Clair's hand.

"I have something to tell you."

Clair knew something was wrong and could see it in her mother's eyes.

She had been relaxed enjoying her snacks, but concern replaced the relaxation, then sat up and asked, "What is it, mother?"

Rae held her hand even tighter... squeezing it.

"I have cancer."

Clair jerked her hand away and scooted to the other side of the sofa.

"What do you mean you have cancer?"

"And they think it has spread. It's not good."

Clair said nothing and could not believe what she heard, sat for a few moments, then crazy arrived.

"This is a joke! Ha, ha. And you said I was the one with a sense of humor."

"Listen, Clair..."

Clair stood up and crossed her arms like a pouting child.

"No! I won't listen! This isn't true!"

"Clair, sit down."

She did, and a dose of hard reality hit her smack dab in the soul. She collapsed on her mother's lap and cried.

Gently caressing her face, Rae said, "Honey, it will be all right."

"How? You even said it wasn't good. That in itself doesn't sound good. Are you going to die?"

"They've been taking excellent care of me at the hospital. I've been taking chemotherapy, but there doesn't seem to be any noticeable progress. To answer your question... who knows?"

Clair tries to make sense of this news. She raised from her mother's lap and sat up.

"I can't believe this is happening," then thought, "*first it was Stanley, now my mom. This death and dying stuff is too much to handle.*"

Clair grabbed her mother's hand one more time and with tears streaming down her face, asked, "What am I supposed to do?"

"Take care of Thomas."

"What about you? What can I do?"

"There is nothing you can do. It all seems like a waste of time and money, but I have a few more rounds of chemo. They think it may buy me some time. You can go with me if you'd like."

"Yes, I will. When?"

"What time is it?"

Clair got dressed, put on a little make-up and the two went out the door.

* * *

The evening Clair got the news of her mother's health, she revisited an old friend; her butcher knife. Her emotions were on full alert, and thoughts from the past ran through her. She was desperate, scared and alone. All the pills and booze were thrown out years ago, and couldn't turn to them—for now.

Clair was in a panic and shouted, "I need to call someone! This is more than I can take!"

She ran to the phone, picked it up and dialed a number. Before anyone could answer, she hung up.

"It's time for me to deal with this," then rummaged through her "tool box" as Glenn referred to it. Clair sat with the knife still in her grasp, studied it and noticed blood stains left behind on the wooden handle. She flipped it from side to side as before, and took the dull side of it and placed it on her arm, then made little sawing motions back and forth.

"This is nuts! This is the old me, not the new one."

She gathered courage then sat it down.

The questions of Clair's past caught up with her.

"*What did I do?*" And, "*Why do I deserve this?*"

She repeated the questions again, then it came to her. It was never two questions; just one.

"*What did I do to deserve this?*"

Yes, many things were done wrong to her, and as a result did many things wrong to others— including herself.

Clair had recited the Serenity Prayer thousands of times but never understood its meaning until now. She knew there were things that can never change, and some that can. For the first time, Clair was aware of the difference, and her mother's illness helped find the answer.

Clair picked the knife back up and gazed at it and recalled the days gone by, but this time pleased at its reflection. She smiled, got out of the chair and placed it back in the drawer. An instant later reopened it, reached in and grabbed the blade and spoke to it.

"You'll never hurt a chicken or me again. Oh, you know what I mean," and tossed it into the trashcan.

"Well, Colonel, it's just you, me and all those herbs and spices from now on."

* * *

Clair had learned many lessons over time, one of them was sharper focus and a deeper understanding of her depression. She also knew this was Rae's challenge and not hers; she was just invited to the dance. All Clair could do for now was to love, support and comfort her mother.

Clair was with her mother night and day for the next several weeks, then Rae's health took a sudden turn and was admitted to the hospital. As soon as Clair got the word of her mother's failing health, canceled the final day of an art show and returned to be with her. When she arrived, the hospital room was crowded with machines and other medical equipment. Clair noticed the IV's stuck in her mother's arms and the heart monitor echoing its endless beeping. Other tubes and a respirator were nearby, and the smell of antiseptic cleaner filled the air, and Thomas was the only one with Rae.

"I'll leave you two alone."

He kissed Rae on the forehead and gave Clair a hug.

Clair went to her mother's bedside. She was weak and short of breath, and her words were labored.

"I don't want you to see me this way. Would you grab my wig?"

"Mom, you look all right."

"Then please get me my hat. I'm cold."

Clair got her hat and placed it on her head.

"Do you like it? It's a Nike."

"It's nice. You look like a golfer."

Clair stood by her side for several minutes trying to hold back tears.

"Clair, since meeting Thomas and reuniting with you, I am the happiest I've been in a long time."

She held Rae's hand, and not able to hold it back, a single tear rolled down Clair's face.

"Me too, mom. Me too."

"Both of you have brought me so much joy."

"I know. Save your strength."

A nurse entered the room.

"Mrs. Reynolds, it's time for your medication."

Rae was growing weary of this twice a day routine, and it showed.

"What is it this time?"

"This will help with the pain and make you sleep."

The nurse gave a single injection into the IV port.

"I'll check back in later."

As the nurse left the room, Rae elevated her voice a notch or two.

"I can't wait. Next time, could we make it a double!"

"Mom, they're just doing their job."

"Clair, I swear to God, these people are turning me into a dope fiend."

"I wouldn't sweat it. When you get out, I'll help you find a support group," — then giggled — "I have a Rolodex full of them. It's been a long day, and I'm tired. It's nappy time."

The hospital made sleeping arrangements for Clair, it wasn't the most comfortable, but it would do. She unfolded the blanket, ruffled her pillow and laid down.

"How was the exhibit?"

Clair let out a big yawn.

"I sold a few pieces. The mayor of Atlanta wants me to paint a portrait of him."

"Are you?"

"I'm not sure, but I think he was hitting on me."

"That's not so bad."

"Mom, he's about eighty years old. I'm going to sleep."

Rae knows Clair is tired and upset and wanted to give her some reassurance.

"This is all part of God's plan."

"I wish He'd give me a heads-up every so often."

Clair had grown a lot the past few years, but unlike before when something went wrong, it was easy to blame herself. Now the question of '*what did I do to deserve this,*' was never a thought anymore, instead rational thinking took over. Whatever pain and suffering her mother was going through was only the tragic circle of life, but even with the justification, it didn't make it any easier... for either one.

Clair was half awake but dozed off. Rae got out of bed, rolled the IV pole along and knelt beside her. The safeness of the sound of Clair's breathing and soft hands against hers gave Rae comfort. She hadn't a clue if Clair was asleep or somewhat conscious, but needed to talk to her.

"Honey, whatever happens, I want you to know how much you mean to me."

Rae continued but heard a quiet snore.

"You couldn't have known, but the first time I ever held you, I wished you a happy birthday."

Clair shifted position in the recliner, and its squeakiness woke her.

"I remember like it was yesterday. It makes me sad that I missed so many of your birthdays."

Still groggy, Clair said, "Don't worry about it, I missed plenty of them myself."

Rae stroked her hair.

"I suppose you have. I love you so much. Go to sleep."

Awakened, but still half asleep, Clair said, "I love you too, mama," then let out another loud yawn.

"You have a big day tomorrow. Go back to bed and rest. Do you need any help?"

"I can manage on my own."

"Okay, mom. I'll see you in the morning."

Rae stroked her hair one last time and thought to herself, "*I hope so.*"

She rubbed Clair's back for a few minutes until she went into a deep sleep. Rae struggled to get to her feet and inched back to bed, crawled in, and prayed in silence.

"God, take care of my little girl and make this pain end."

She was exhausted, then took a long, strenuous breath and ended her prayer with a request. Her final prayer was that during sleep, she'd have beautiful dreams. Rae took another breath and fell asleep. During her slumber, her prayer was answered.

Throughout Rae's time at the hospital, Clair and Thomas became the best of friends, and their friendship strengthened. He was not only a good companion, but in a lot of ways he became her surrogate father. It was though her mother stepped aside and allowed another to take her place.

Chapter XVII

Clair chose the five-year anniversary of Stanley's death to visit him. Though she had never been to his grave site and didn't attend the funeral, today seemed like a special occasion. It was a somber, gloomy, cloudy afternoon, almost winter, with drizzle mixed with sleet. She had a grave map and wandered around for some time looking for it. Beyond a small hill, she noticed a bird flying in a tight circle.

"It couldn't be. Okay, Stanley, I'll bite."

She walked over where the bird had been flying and there it was: his monument. It was a small, rectangular granite stone buried in the ground. At the top was a carved image of Jesus, his name, and date of birth; absent was the day of death. There was a simple inscription below:

Here lies one of God's angels and angels never die.

Clair believed guardian angels were a myth, but now felt there was no doubt they existed. Fighting back tears, she sat near his grave and spoke to him.

"I will love you forever."

She remained with him for several more hours like she did when watching him sleep.

"I figured I'd find you here."

She stood up, brushed herself off, and wiped a single tear.

"Oh, Hi Glenn. Yeah, I wanted to come and see Stanley. It's been a while."

"I know, me too. I haven't been back since the funeral."

She knelt again in front of the grave marker and cleared away a few fallen leaves.

"It's beautiful."

"It's simple — that was his wish. Dad had an expensive one picked out, but he wanted the extra money donated to the home for the others. It was a chunk of change."

"He always thought of others." said, Clair.

Glenn reached for her hand and helped her up.

"I couldn't go; it was just too hard. I hope you understand."

"I do."

They walked through the cemetery, and Glenn started some idle chat.

"You changed your hair."

She fluffed it and shook her head to readjust it.

"What do you think?"

He looked it over and gazed at it from side to side.

"I like it."

"I saw Pulp Fiction last summer and figured it was time for a change."

They kept the slow pace, and after a thirty-minute stroll, they got back to Stanley.

"I heard several people attended the funeral, and that the service was very sweet."

"It did, and it was."

Then he chuckled.

"What's so funny?"

"He loved Barry Manilow and insisted they play 'Daybreak.' They did, and everyone thought it was nice. Afterward, there were a few words from the priest, then more Daybreak. We figured it was a mistake, and perhaps the sound guy forgot to play a different one."

She perked up a little.

"Sounds like an honest mistake."

"It gets better. There were two songs left in the service. Guess what the next one was?"

"I give up."

"Daybreak. The crowd laughed a little, along with some quiet chatter."

Glenn was laughing so hard; it was difficult to get the words out.

"After the priest gave a brief sermon and a final sign of the cross —one more song."

Clair laughed too.

"Let me guess —Daybreak?"

His laughter stopped, and so did hers. Glenn and Clair looked into each other's eyes, both sets flowing a river of tears.

They reached for one another and fell into an embrace, and he whispered, "Yes, Daybreak."

The two stayed together for the next several minutes never letting go. Glenn felt comfortable, and Clair felt safe. They were still in each other's arms, and Glenn tried to reach around to wipe his nose.

He was still sniffling and said, "Alrighty then."

He let her go and asked if she wanted to get a cup of coffee.

"Are you asking me on a date?"

"No, just coffee."

Clair lowered herself to the ground and placed fresh-cut flowers on Stanley's grave. She kissed her index and middle fingers and planted them on his marker.

"I'll see you next time."

Glenn helped her up, and they went to their cars. He opened the door for her like a perfect gentleman. Before she got in, he reached for her arm.

"There is something I've been meaning to tell you."

"What is it?"

He squirmed, and thought, "*Feel the fear and just say it,*" then fidgeted his words.

"Well... I'm not too sure how to say it... but..."

He squirmed even more.

"But what?"

He squirmed even more.

"I like you."

"That's it?"

She gave him a quick pat on the back and in a casual tone, said, "I like you too."

He cleared his throat.

"I don't think you understand. I like you a lot and have for years. The truth is, soon after we met. I couldn't get you out of my mind."

Clair was not aware where this was going but had an idea.

Beads of sweat trickled from his forehead, and like a teenage boy, said, "What I am trying to say is that I like... like... like you. You know, the 'big like' "

She repeated him.

"Like... like."

"Yeah, a bunch."

He pulled out a handkerchief and padded his brow.

"I'm burning up. Are you hot?"

"Glenn, it's forty degrees."

She walked around him and leaned against the hood of the car. There was a crack in the clouds, and the sun shined on her face and used her hand as a visor. Clair stood there and thought for a moment. Continuing to shield her eyes turned toward Glenn. She stared him down and seemed a little upset.

"Why didn't you ever tell me?"

"Because I was your therapist; we're taught not to like our clients. I don't mean we can't be empathetic or even sympathetic, and besides, it's a huge no-no. Licenses have flown out the nearest window when counselors got too involved."

He leaned over the hood, and in his usual nerdy self, winked an eye and said, "If you catch my drift."

"Makes sense. You sure have a way with words."

She pushed herself from the car, stood in front of him, face to face. And with a cheeky grin, she said, "You're not my counselor now."

He returned the grin and said, "Nope. Are you in a big hurry?"

"No, I'm not. Why?"

"Me either. There is a 'crick' beyond the parking area. You want to see it?"

"A what?" She said with a giggle.

"Excuse me, sometimes I forget where I am. Let me start over. Do you want to see...?" then emphasized and stretched out his words, "... *a creeeek?*"

"Much better, and yes that would be great."

They walked across the parking lot, and on the way, unknown to Glenn, she made fun of him.

"Now, exactly where are you from?"

"Pennsylvania. Why?"

"Just curious."

The jab flew over him. They made the short journey, and at the edge of the parking lot, there was a small pathway within the tall brush and shrubbery. At the end of the trail, was a narrow stream of water, complete with a downed tree that served as a bridge.

"Let's cross it!"

Glenn obliged but said to himself, "It looked a lot bigger when I was a kid."

It was narrow and wide enough for one at a time, then she reached for his hand.

"Come on! Follow me!"

When they got to the other side, she didn't let go, and neither did he.

"Now that we're here, I want to show you something else."

Glenn led the way, and a few steps were the wooden remains of a small structure.

"This is what's left of a fort Stanley and I built when we were kids."

"You used to be a kid?"

Teasing him again, she said, "I figured you popped out of the womb as a full-grown adult."

"Not really, I did it the regular way. Got born, learned to walk and talk, then went to college."

"What about the stuff in the middle?"

"That's a different story. You know about my mother, I'll tell you the rest later, but not now."

They spent a while looking at the scenery. Clair picked up a small pebble and tried to skip it across the creek; it went plop and sank. She sat beside Glenn with little distance between them.

"I'm curious. Why did you become a counselor?"

"In high school, I was much of a nothing; I didn't fit in with the crowd. We had the socials, freaks, and goat-ropers. I couldn't afford to keep up with the socials, didn't do drugs, and don't own a cowboy hat, but I was on the debate team."

"I bet you were a pro at that."

"No, I wasn't. I don't like to argue. But I was the one everyone came to with a problem and seemed to have a knack for it and gave most of the right answers. In my senior year, a light went off. I figured handing out advice was a good thing, so I should get paid for it. So, I went to college, got my counseling degree, then a masters, and now I'm working on my Ph.D."

"Very impressive, Dr. Glenn."

"I guess so. Counseling doesn't pay much, but it keeps the bill collectors away; besides, I like helping people."

Glenn continued.

"Aside from the stuff that was going on in your life, I know little about you. What do you do for fun?"

"I love my work as an artist, but I also like to play tennis, go camping with friends, and rock climb."

"Rock climbing? Weren't you afraid of falling?"

She glared at him.

"Me? Scared of falling? You have got to be joking!"

Glenn let out a hint of a laugh.

"I guess you're right. You did become the group expert."

"Yeah, I suppose I did. You know a few more things about me. What about you? What do you do for fun?"

"Me and some of the gang play bridge during lunch at the center."

"*Oooh*, that's sounds exciting. Do you have to wear padded protection?"

"No, just regular clothes."

"It was a joke."

"Oh, I get it. Ha. Before you make too much fun of it, a bridge game can get nasty. I yelled once."

"Wow."

Then she thought, "*He really is a nerd, but still cute.*"

"I'm also taking tennis lessons. Maybe I'll get good enough to challenge you to a match."

"Get good quick. I was number one on my high-school tennis team my junior and senior year. I was also offered a college scholarship to play."

Glenn lowered his head and said, "Great."

Then he perked up.

"Do you want to learn how to play bridge?"

She placed one finger under her chin, looked up and said, "Let me think."

About two seconds later looked back at him.

"Okay, I thought about it. No!"

"I can't say I blame you. Hell, I'm not sure why I play. My parents played all the time and taught me the game, now it's only something to do."

Glenn took a firm stance and stood his ground.

"From now on, no more bridge. I'm sticking to tennis."

Clair warned, "It can be dangerous."

"I don't care. I'm throwing caution to the wind and take a risk and doubling my tennis lessons starting this week." Then he mimicked a sweeping tennis racquet back and forth.

"Oh great, I've created a monster."

It was getting late, and they had to go. Glenn and Clair crossed back over the log, but this time, he led. They held hands every step of the way to her car. Again, he opened the door, and before stepping in, Clair moved in close to Glenn, put both arms around him and gave him a little peck on the lips.

"Why don't we get that cup of coffee and see where this goes."

* * *

They dated for a few months, and one evening after a quiet dinner, Glenn placed a small wrapped gift box beside her plate.

"This is a surprise. What is it?"

"Guess."

"A pony?"

"You're close. Guess again. Never mind, just open it."

She did, and it was empty.

"I don't get it."

Glenn reached into his shirt pocket, got down on one knee, and placed a small engagement ring on her finger.

"Will you?"

Clair gazed into his eyes with more intensity than ever before. She wasn't thinking or confused about an answer; just taking in the moment. A happy tear rolled down her face that signaled her answer.

Clair took a chance and let another one in. Six months later they got married, and Thomas made sure it was a lavish wedding. Lots of invitations and a lot of guests. Big cake, big dress, big reception, and to top it off — a big limo. Glenn was comfortable with all the extravagance except for the fancy car and put his foot down; his Plymouth was all right with him. Clair had other plans, and after a brief discussion, Glenn agreed. They took the limousine.

* * *

Near the beginning of the service, the priest asked, "Who gives this woman to be married to this man?"

Arm in arm, Thomas responded.

"Her mother and I."

He kissed Clair on the cheek and whispered, "We love you so much. Have a wonderful life."

He left her side, and Glenn took over. Rae sat on the front row and was grinning from ear-to-ear. Her cancer scare was in the past and was in full remission.

Funny moments at a wedding aren't rare, although this one got everyone laughing out loud, including Thomas, Rae and the bridal trio. At the end of the ceremony, right after "you may kiss the bride," the priest introduced the couple.

"Ladies and gentlemen, I'd like to introduce Glenn Paulston Bayer and his new bride."

Glenn requested the priest to not use his middle name, but he either forgot, or it fell on deaf ears. Glenn was paralyzed where he stood.

Clair turned to him and whispered, "Paulston?"

Stone-faced and speechless, he ignored her and stared straight ahead.

Before the wedding, Clair dropped her maiden name and used Glenn's —a decision she humorously regretted.

"And now may I introduce the new bride...."

In a flash, she yelled in her head, "*Oh my God!*"

Then here it came, "... Mrs. Clair Bayer."

This time, Glenn turned toward her.

"Clair Bayer?"

The three were petrified, staring motionless toward the crowd. There was not the usual applause from the guests; they were stunned too. By this time, the priest was getting loopy from all the wine.

He gulped down the last of it, tilted his head between them, chuckled, and whispered, "Sounds like a stuffed animal. Get it? Care Bear, Clair Bayer."

Trying to keep a straight face, she whispered, "Yes, Father, we get it."

His comment got the two grinning, but he also forgot to turn off his microphone; then came a round of applause and roaring laughter... and the three at the altar as well joined in the laughter.

Yes, her name sounded funny to all, but it was the sweetest one in the world, at least to her.

Conclusion

It was a beautiful Sunday morning, and the weather was perfect. The sun rose from the east, and a warm breeze blew from the west. Clair spent the time picking flowers and pruning her plants. Glenn came out juggling a tray of iced lemonade in one hand, two tumblers in the other, and a tennis racket tucked under his arm. He placed the tray and its contents on a nearby table, gave her a peck on the cheek, and was off to play tennis with his buddies.

Clair stood beside him and said, "I have an idea."

"What is it?"

"Why don't you invite a few of your OCD group members over next weekend?"

"My, who?"

"Your compulsive, disorder clients. We'll have a cook-out," —then whispered — "and see who wants to help clean the house."

"Oh, yeah. I'm sure it would be fun, and they would do a great job, but, Clair, do you think that's a good idea?"

She laughed, "Probably not."

"Well, I need to skedaddle."

"Wait a minute."

Before he left, she put her arms around his neck and hugged him so hard, he feared it would cut blood flow to his brain. Cheek-to-cheek, she whispered in his ear.

"You saved my life."

154

He moved away and cupped her face with both hands.

"No, Clair, you did."

Again, she wrapped her arms around him.

"I love you so much."

"Me too, sweetheart."

He kissed her again, this time, right on the mouth.

As Clair continued to heal physically and mentally, she realized it wasn't just the marriage that helped her; it was the crème de la crème. After he left, and for a few moments, thought about his words. He was right; Clair had saved her own life. She held her arms out straight, palms down and turned them over. Her scars were healed and served as a reminder of the torn days left behind.

The day was getting warmer, and she was a little tired. Clair made herself comfortable on a lawn chair next to the tray and poured a glass of the refreshing drink. She was relaxed, took a sip, and daydreamed.

As she was drifting off, thought to herself, "*I now have a mortgage, a husband, bills, two cats and a dog —*" then felt a little kick and rubbed her swollen belly.

"Today is a good day to be alive."

For years, Clair had hoped her make believe dreams would come true, but now she was old enough to know fairy tales weren't real. Glenn was not a prince, nor she a princess, but with tarnished and dented armor and her dress tattered and torn, Glenn was still her knight, and Clair was his damsel in distress. It wasn't Camelot, but it was good enough for her.

Epilogue

Childhood is supposed to be carefree, innocent and filled with an abundance of love. Nothing is free, but in the long-run, being a kid is expected to be made that way —if you were one of the fortunate ones.

There are many of us out there who can concur that their life started out much like Clair's —chaotic, frightening and immersed in utter pandemonium. What a great way to start life —I do not think so. It dictates the path we choose in our existence —how we feel and treat ourselves and others.

While editing Suicide by Death, I grew increasingly tied to the main character, Clair. I know editors are not supposed to get involved with the 'players', but I did. It turns out Clair and I have a lot in common —and I became her passionate advocate —her mirror image so to speak. There were times I wanted to step inside Clair's world and protect her, do a little physical damage to those who caused her so much pain and angst. It tore open personal wounds, which I thought were dealt with long ago. I realize now there are scars that can still bleed; sometimes profusely. You can attain all the counseling you want, but they are still there corked down so deeply that when they surface, you want to scream or do something irrational to quell the anger and bitterness built up within ourselves.

The first example in our lives is our family. If you cannot trust them to love and support you, then who can you trust? Inevitably, we end up attracting or being attracted to the same toxicity throughout the rest of our lives. We learned it when our early years were full of emotional insanity — and think we are moving forward, all the while we go through the motions and try to discover what love really is. All of us know how to spell it, but what is it in the real sense of the word? If we do not have positive examples of a functional start in life, it is hit and miss —and most times a miss.

When innocence is taken from us so early in life, it becomes an awkward jigsaw puzzle of choices, like pulling a rabbit out of an arena full of hats. Sometimes we get lucky, sometimes not, and it is usually the 'not' that is the winner in the quest for happiness and self-awareness. One can move on and catch whatever prism as it shines its light on you. Nevertheless, the damage is there to stay. It is what we do with it that counts.

People like Clair would look at a relationship and ask, "If he likes me, there must be something wrong with him." I call it the "Damaged Goods Syndrome." We feel we are undeserving of love or happiness. It was beaten into us subtly so early on. Too many times it is unsalvageable. It is the hamster wheel that keeps on spinning. In the end, the lucky ones survive and have content lives. Sure, we can continue wandering down a path of self-destruction and self-loathing and hope for the best, or let nature take its course and take what you get. Sometimes you win — sometimes you do not.

As I read through the book, I found myself re-gluing myself emotionally back together in small ways, but they all added up. "If Clair can do it, so can I." I can honestly say after closing the book, I felt different somehow. I saw my own demons in a different light as Clair did. Things did not seem so hopeless any longer, and I've been looking for it my entire life. Sometimes it takes that one person to point the way, and in creating the characters in Suicide by Death, I want to thank Mark for brilliantly assembling some sort of sanity out of the emotional rubble for me.

Quite honestly, I will miss Clair. I wish her the best.
Carla Michale Clark

Author notes

In my first book, Three Days in Heaven, my author notes were practically a chapter! This one will be short and to the point.

Today I read a quote written by "unknown," and it went like this;

On particularly rough days when I'm sure I can't possibly endure,
I like to remind myself that my track record for getting through bad
days so far is 100%... and that's pretty good.

Suicide is the tenth leading cause of death in the U.S., some studies say it's the ninth. Regardless, it's too many. Whatever the ranking, it impacts millions of friends, families, co-workers and colleagues every year. I spent many hours researching this topic and became somewhat educated. I am not a psychiatrist, psychologist, or even a mental health expert, but I owned and operated a drug and alcohol counseling practice for many years, so I do have some insight. I know this for sure: if you have ever thought about hurting or killing yourself, do us a favor and get help, and if you know someone you suspect has tried, urge them to get help as well. It might offend them, but guess what? I would rather piss off an alive friend or relative who got help than have ignored the warning signs of a dead one.

If you or someone you know needs help or assistance, please call:
National Suicide Prevention Lifeline
(800) 273-8255 Hours: 24 hours, 7 days a week
Languages: English, Spanish

Website: www.SuicidePreventionLifeline.org
For more information about depression, visit WebMD at www.webmd.com/depression/guide

Made in the
USA
Monee, IL